He was there to protect them—
even if he had to kill them

He believed in the old blood codes of justice.
He'd break any law to fight the lawless.
He was the people's champion—yet their most
    dangerous enemy.
Was he a new breed of avenger?
Or a coldblooded killer?

THE PROTECTOR

THE PROTECTOR

MALCOLM BRALY

Based on a screenplay by
RICHARD LEVINSON & WILLIAM LINK

J

A JOVE BOOK

Printed in the United States of America

First Jove edition published September 1979

10   9   8   7   6   5   4   3   2   1

Jove books are published by Jove Publications, Inc., 200 Madi-
son Avenue, New York, NY 10016.

THE PROTECTOR

CHAPTER ONE

When Charlie Hyatt first thought back to mark the afternoon it all began, he remembered how he had worked later than usual and got caught in the heart of the rush. The transition from his office, high in Rockefeller Center, to the subway platform 50 feet below the building was always wrenching, even at 2:30, but by 5:30 when Charlie finally got away the crowd was boiling through the cement passageways. A living underground river of cells drawn from every organ in the city. Down here the distinctions of class were meaningless. As soon as he was jammed in the car, against a robust woman in a black coat on one side and a Filipino in a green parka on the other, Charlie became freight. No one looked at anyone else. All these people crammed in here tighter than pigs penned for shipping were determined to remain strangers. Charlie swayed with the car, feeling the weight of his briefcase, studied the ads he had studied before, and tried to recall the subway as it had seemed when he had lived in the Village and rode up at night to see double bills in the westside art houses. He knew the subway had been no different then. He was different now.

He was a success. Success in the Village meant you could move to the upper westside, because it was better for the kids. You could cab to the Village at night to drink with old friends. But after a while you didn't go so much. When had they started to slow down? he mused with a kind of gentle wonder. It was the baby-sitters probably. There was always a problem. Well, he didn't mind that, except he felt different. He knew he acted much the same and friends were always telling him how well he looked, but in the center something was different. Something was less, and on top of that the westside was starting to turn sour.

He came to the surface at Broadway and Seventy-second Street, and directly behind him was the patch of dried grass and ring of benches known as Needle Park. Even tourists knew heroin was on sale here. In the streets around there were 1000s of people who took drugs as a way of life, drugs were their basic commodity, and every cliche of the black marketplace was harshly aggravated. The whole island was grossly over-crowded and the streets everywhere were jammed with poor and powerless people. You didn't have to be a sociology professor to know the crunch was on and those it hurt the most were those who could afford it least. Charlie could smell it changing down here in the streets. He still enjoyed the New York streets as a great life spectacle, but he tended to walk faster these days.

He crossed Broadway and headed down his own sidestreet toward the Hudson River. He lived in one of the smaller of these red-brick apartment buildings, raised in the 20s to provide riverview apartments for a newly affluent middle class, and his place was one of the great scores of his life. The rooms were huge, he had 12 foot ceilings and Georgian beams. On clear days he could see New Jersey from his bedroom windows. Best of all, it was rent controlled. On an open market, Charlie's apartment would go for $1200. He paid $375, and that difference helped him overlook the trouble he sensed brewing in the streets.

In front of his own building, he found Morrison walking his dog. The dog was a muscular shorthair whose naked balls annoyed Charlie, and Morrison was a tall man with rounded shoulders and pitted cheeks, who looked like he still used Vitalis. Charlie hardly knew him. Charlie had tried some jokes on him once or twice and he had been sure Morrison was only smiling because he knew it was expected. Today Charlie said, "How's it going?"

And Morrison said, "Not bad." Before he looked back at his dog, who was beginning to deposit a large coil of yellow shit.

Charlie let himself in, glanced at a package on the mail table to see that it was for Dr. and Mrs. Philip Julian, and ran upstairs to his own apartment on the second floor. The phone was ringing when he came in, and he yelled automatically "I'll get it," not even sure Lynn was home. Then he heard her in the kitchen.

"Why are you so late?"

"Just more of the same happy horseshit," he said

9

and picked up the phone. It was Richard. Charlie braced himself and began to listen to Richard explain why the scripts weren't ready. He smiled despite himself because Richard saved his best fantasies for these necessary explanations. He stood at the window, watching a large orange cat sitting in another window across the street. He heard Robbie come in, slamming the door, resetting the Foxx lock with a casual swing of his foot. Then his kid came slumping into the living room, pretending to be exhausted. He tossed his books on the couch, added his clarinet case, and shucked his jacket to throw on top.

Charlie yelled, "Put that stuff in your room."

On the phone, he heard Richard falter. "Not you," Charlie said, "That was my kid."

Today Richard had discovered there wasn't a single character in *Under the Same Sky*, not even Mr. Angus, the postman, who only walked through several times a year, whose motivation made any sense. There wasn't a shred of consistency in any character. Charlie knew it was true enough, and so had Richard, when he took the job. Charlie stopped him now.

"Listen, Richard, let's cut to the nut. I've got to have those pages tomorrow and I mean *ee-rye* in the morning. I wish we were the Peetown Playhouse, but we're not, and this cast can't be expected to ad lib its way out of trouble. So it's do-or-die time. Sit right down and hit it."

It was a moment before Richard said, "Sure—" In a tone so swollen with reluctance, Charlie could hear the "but" that was coming next.

"Good!" Charlie said quickly and hung up like he was snapping down the lid on a basketfull of snakes.

He stood where he was, thinking about Richard. He knew Richard spent his nights in Village bars talking

10

out the plays he was going to write. Most mornings he had the shakes and usually he didn't get to work, if he wrote at all, until late afternoon. Then he sneered at the work that bought his bread and booze. Why can't I find an honest hack? Charlie wondered.

He heard Lynn greeting Robbie in the kitchen. "How was practice?" she asked.

Robbie said, "Shitty."

"Robbie! Can't you find another word?"

"That's the word I hear all the time."

Charlie walked into the kitchen to find the two of them looking at each other over the table set for dinner. Lynn was staring at Robbie, testing his last statement for insolence, and Robbie was projecting as much innocence as he could manage.

"What was wrong with practice?" Charlie asked, ignoring the other subject.

Robbie made a face of comic disgust. "Oh, Mr. Wilson had us playing some moldy oldie for over half the hour."

"Did it have a name?" Charlie asked.

"To a Wildrose."

Charlie smiled with a conscious self-mockery. "I used to like that."

Robbie knew his lines. "That's because you're a cornball, Dad," he said.

Charlie's corniness was a family legend, one he stoked himself, and it amused him to allow Robbie to imagine he had spent his youth smoking mentholated cigarettes, sipping sweet red wine, and listening to Johnny Ray records, all of which had led naturally to his job as director of *Under the Same Sky,* which they agreed was the silliest show on the box.

Lynn was saying, "He needs reeds again."

Charlie glanced at his wife. Lynn had a small mole

11

just above her upper lip. When he was happy with her this birthmark seemed the perfect punctuation of her beauty. When he was irritated it became a witch's wart. Just now it was the former. He realized the better part of a week had slipped by since they had last made love. Married sex was so often a matter of timing.

Robbie was talking about his reeds. "I split my last good one, and the rest are turkeys."

"Do you know what those reeds are starting to cost?" Charlie asked.

Robbie shrugged; his eyes had slipped away. He wasn't ready to start thinking about what things cost.

Charlie continued: "Can't you use a plastic reed?"

"Sure, Dad," Robbie said scornfully, "I might as well start playing the kazoo."

Charlie smiled, despite himself. Still, he was determined to give Robbie some sense of prudence. If the future turned out to be harsher than the present, he didn't want his son to be helpless. "Then you should learn to cut your own reeds. I'll get you the stuff you'll need."

"Dad, you've said that before."

"I know. It's time now."

"Sit down, you guys," Lynn said, as she turned from the stove with a hot casserole in her hands. "Robbie, take some beans and pass them."

Robbie took three green beans and put them on his plate as if he thought they might explode. He stared at them a moment, then apparently decided he couldn't get by with so few, because he carefully took two more before he passed the bowl to Charlie. Charlie sat holding the beans while he savored the feel of his family. For a moment his life was briefly like clear water. Then he started to help himself, pausing while

Lynn put a ham steak on his plate, before he finished taking what he wanted. He was putting the bowl near Lynn's place when he heard a sharp slapping sound.

"What the hell was that?" he asked softly.

He caught Lynn's eye and saw the mirror of his own instinctive alarm. "A backfire?" she suggested.

Robbie was immediately up and looking out the window at the street below.

"Robbie!" Charlie was surprised at the crack of his own voice. "Sit down and stay down!" He turned to Lynn. "Cars almost never backfire anymore. And besides, I think it came from out there." He pointed toward the outside hallway. "I'd better take a look."

"Charlie, *don't!*" Lynn said.

He stared at her a moment, sensing her alarm, before he said again, "I'd better."

Lynn turned on Robbie. "Robbie, you go right to your room, and stay there. Don't come out for anything."

As Charlie walked quietly and quickly to his own front door, he heard the sharp clatter of leather heels on the marble stairway that led down into the small lobby. Two, maybe three people running downstairs. He leaned over and put his eye to the tiny spyhole, but he saw only the oyster-colored wall of the hall corridor. Somehow that bland expanse of wall only deepened his sense of alarm, and then he heard something—a muffled thump on his own door—and carefully pulled the police lock aside. The brass fittings slid in their slots with a faintly greasy click.

"Charlie!" Lynn whispered urgently just behind him.

"Someone's out there, I think . . ."

When he fully released the second lock, some pressure began to push the door in toward him, and

he had just barely stepped aside when a man fell into
their apartment with the slow, effortless sprawl of
someone tumbling underwater. The man had been sitting on the floor, leaning against their door. He wore
only a bright blue pair of boxer shorts, and his face
was covered with a red foam that looked almost like
strawberries and whipped cream. Charlie recognized
the clumps of rusty orange hair and the faded blue
chain tattooed around the left wrist. It was . . . it had
been Wallace, from the fourth floor. Charlie became
aware that someone was standing on the stairs just
above him, screaming.

It was Sarah Wallace, and she was staring at the
ruin that had been her husband's face. Charlie turned
to Lynn. She was also staring down at Wallace. Her
eyes were wide with shock, and she had stuck one fist
in her open mouth. "Call the police," Charlie said.
Then, with great reluctance, he knelt over Wallace to
see if there was anything he could do.

Later, Charlie stood in his own kitchen, along with
a Lieutenant Yeager and two carfuls of precinct cops,
and listened while Sarah Wallace told what had happened. She sat at the table, and as she spoke, she continued to rub her face again and again, massaging it
harshly as if to erase something. A cup of instant
Lynn had mixed for her stood untouched. For the first
time in weeks, Charlie yearned for a smoke. He stood
sensing that familiar dry tension in his throat, as he
watched Lieutenant Yeager writing swiftly in a small
spiral notebook. Whenever Sarah Wallace faltered,
Yeager asked her another question, and she wound
on, speaking with obvious misery, scrubbing at her
face.

Paul, Mr. Wallace, had been shaving for dinner;

they were going out, and she was waiting at the kitchen table, looking through a magazine that had come that day. When the knock came, she had simply assumed it was Mrs. Jacobs down the hall. Mrs. Jacobs often looked in—they were friends, and she often needed to borrow a bit of this or a little of that—and besides, Sarah hadn't buzzed anyone through the downstairs front door, so it never occurred to her it could be anybody else, and she unfastened the chain without looking.

The two boys came in fast. One black, one Puerto Rican, and they looked like the characters she saw outside on the street, with neck chains and big silver buckles. One of them had grabbed her, spun her around, and locked his forearm over her throat. It must have been the Puerto Rican, because she remembered the black boy going through her purse. It was right on the table, because they were going out.

If only God had given her the sense not to scream, those boys would simply have taken the few dollars she had and run away with them, but, no, like a foolish old chicken, her mind blazed with alarm and she was screaming before she could even think. And then Paul, Mr. Wallace, was running in, as mad as she had ever seen him, like a runaway engine, just wild with anger, and the black boy was suddenly waving a small silver gun, calling him terrible names, but it made no difference. He threw the boys out bodily, and that might have satisfied him if he hadn't noticed her open purse.

By now she had collected her wits, and she tried to tell him the boys hadn't taken anything, but he didn't believe her. He grabbed her purse and dumped it on the table, and because she always carried this big red

wallet he had given her three years ago for her birth-
day, he knew right away it was gone. He started out
after those boys. She followed in a panic, yelling for
him to come back. Then she heard angry shouting below, and the shot sounded hollow as a cannon in the
stairwell.

Charlie Hyatt could imagine the rest of this brief
and deadly story. He hadn't known Wallace, except
to nod to him in the hall, but he had been aware of
the other man's anger. Wallace had been one of those
large redheaded people with thick white skin, and
even far gone in middle age he had still moved with a
suggestive lightness and his flat green eyes had often
seemed sullen. He gave the impression of a former
street kid who had been tough enough to fight his
way into the upper middle class but had never come
to feel easy there. And his anger, and whatever else it
was besides the natural imperative to protect his
home, had driven Wallace, barefoot and naked except
for his shorts, his face still lathered with shaving
cream, down to the second-floor landing in front of
Charlie Hyatt's door, where one of those two kids had
shot him right beside the nose. All that anger had
winked out.

Lieutenant Yeager went over the description of the
two boys again and again, trying to prompt Sarah
Wallace into recovering more detail, and to Charlie
the makes sounded like half the kids he saw standing
around the sidewalks out on Broadway—any of them
or all of them. But Yeager seemed satisfied. He passed
his notes to one of the precinct cops and said, "Get
this right out." Then he turned to Charlie and continued, "They're an unusual pair, and they just copped
for a few bucks—we might spot them trying to spend it.

"Do you think they were junkies?" Charlie asked.

16

Yeager's eyes flickered. "Maybe. It's a place to start."

Watching Yeager work had caused Charlie to realize how much his expectation of police lieutenants had been based on various fictions. The same actors played cops again and again, and no matter what kind of cops they pretended to be, there was always a certain theatrical flair that was entirely missing from this real cop. Yeager could have been here to make an estimate for repairs to the plumbing. His suit was too tight, his hat too small, and his light tan eyes were utterly neutral.

"Tell me again what you saw and heard, and don't leave anything out," Yeager said, and Charlie recalled the brief scene, trying to remember everything except Wallace's face as he fell through the door. Then Yeager asked Lynn the same question, and Charlie went into the living room and poured himself a half tumbler of straight Scotch and drank it off. The question that interested him most was one Yeager hadn't asked. What would he, Charlie Mason Hyatt, have done in Wallace's place? Wallace was a fool who had thrown his life away, but wasn't there something to admire in his brute courage? The thought made Charlie feel pale and timid.

The men from the meat wagon were zipping Wallace's corpse into a body bag, and Rudy Simbro, the super, was waiting to mop up. Charlie became aware that a number of residents were standing outside on the stairs, talking in subdued tones. When the body was gone, Dr. Phil Julian walked in, and old Mr. Jacobs and Chambers from the third floor crowded in behind him. "Charlie, are you all right?" Dr. Julian asked.

Charlie nodded. "Can I give anyone a drink?"

"Yes, please," Julian said, and Mr. Jacobs asked, "Did you see them?"

"No, I heard them on the stairs." He poured more of the Scotch for Dr. Julian and hit himself again. Lieutenant Yeager came in, still holding his notebook, and Charlie shook the bottle in mute offering, but Yeager declined.

"What I want to know," Julian said, "is how'd they get in? This building's supposed to be secure, isn't it?"

Yeager answered. "Someone probably buzzed them in. These kind of kids aren't schooled thieves, you know, they just look around until they find a soft spot. They come in behind someone, catch the door before it closes, or they get someone to buzz them in without calling down to see who it is."

Charlie volunteered. "Our call system doesn't work anyway."

Yeager looked surprised. "Why not?"

"This is a rent-controlled building, and the owners claim they don't make enough to cover the cost of maintenance."

Yeager's expression changed to one of exasperation. "You can report this to the city housing authority. That works, you know, they really ride the owners, and if they don't comply they're quick to fine them."

"We know that," Charlie agreed, "and they fix it every five or six months, but it goes right out again. The whole system needs to be replaced."

"What's the matter with those people?" Dr. Julian said angrily. "They're counting pennies and meanwhile a life has been lost. Jesus, Charlie, they could have hit your place, or mine."

That was really it, Charlie thought.

"This used to be a nice neighborhood," Mr. Jacobs said heavily. "A very nice place to live, and now I'm afraid to let Mrs. Jacobs go to the market alone, and now—now I won't even be able to leave her alone in our apartment. What can we do?"

That question became the theme of the impromptu tenants' meeting that was held in Charlie Hyatt's apartment. The residents gathered to console Sarah Wallace and stayed to talk over their problem with Lieutenant Yeager. Charlie offered drinks to everyone and took several more himself, until the awful event began to grow smaller in his mind, and then went from room to room gathering chairs. He found Robbie still in his bedroom, lying on his bed sideways with his feet up on the wall between the *Star Wars* poster and another poster of the Orion nebula. His music stand was set up to hold the H. Klosé clarinet method, and his toy box, the same toy box he had had since the summer he was four, was piled high with model cars and planes.

"Can I come out, Dad?"

"I don't see why not, but stay out of the way—we're having a kind of meeting."

Robbie rolled over and stood up, nodding alertly. "Because of that dude upstairs getting iced?"

"Robert! Mr. Wallace has been shot to death, and that's very different from a dude getting iced."

Robbie immediately lowered his head, as he always did when Charlie spoke sharply to him, and Charlie knew he had overreacted because of his own anxiety. He put his arms around his son, and said, "What happened was an awful thing, and it affects all of us. What if they had forced their way in here, and hurt one of us?" He knew it was unfair, and useless as well, to try to force Robbie to imagine things he had never experienced. It couldn't be real to him. He

19

picked those expressions up at school and repeated them without understanding what they really meant.

"Come on," he said, squeezing Robbie's shoulder, "help me get all the chairs into the living room."

Robbie looked up, gratefully, and for a moment he reminded Charlie of Lynn as she had been that first summer. The same clear gray eyes. Robbie was eleven, so she had been eighteen. For a moment he stood back then. His mind played such tricks, and the essence of the past went through him like a sudden wind that was gone almost as soon as he noticed it.

"I'll get this one, Dad," Robbie said, taking the chair from in front of his school desk.

There were two more chairs in their own bedroom, but still not nearly enough, because by now almost all the tenants in the whole building had squeezed into their living room. He saw people he hardly knew. The three girls who lived together on the fifth floor, and Fran Jeffries from the third floor rear. Mrs. Jacobs had joined her husband, and Dr. Julian's wife, Claire, was here, as well as the young couple from the third floor. The name beside their bell read simply MURPHY. The husband held a sleepy child who might have been either a boy or a girl. Morrison stood leaning against the wall. Yeager was sitting at a card table Lynn had set up. He had removed his hat and placed it on the table, and his radio, turned low, sat beside it. The just-audible voices on the police band brought the violent life of the city among them and reminded them they were now a part of it.

Lynn was making coffee in their party urn. Charlie asked her, "Where's Mrs. Wallace?"

"She went upstairs to lie down."

"Alone?"

20

"No, Lisa Chambers went with her. Do you think we should take up a collection to help her out?"

"I don't know. It would only be a gesture. Can I help you?"

Lynn shook her head slightly. "No, I've got it under control."

Charlie knew Lynn had thrown herself into this work to postpone the moment when she would have to begin to consider what had happened. He stepped back into the living room, where Mrs. Jacobs was talking in a soft, hesitant voice, which still held the hint of an accent. She and her husband had lived in the building over thirty years and raised three children here. The two boys had lived with them until they had graduated from Columbia, a few blocks away. Like her husband, Mrs. Jacobs couldn't understand what had happened. "This used to be such a nice neighborhood, it was a pleasure to walk through . . ." She looked around to make sure everyone understood her, then turned back to Lieutenant Yeager. "It's hard to know what's happened. The streets are like a jungle. For ten years it's been getting worse and worse out there. I don't dare go to the market by myself, but at least I thought we were safe in our own building—"

Morrison suddenly interrupted. "What stops those kids from coming back?"

Fran Jeffries, who was a defender of practically everything, was quick to jump Morrison. "Hey," she said to him, "the lady has the floor."

"No, I'm through. I didn't have anything more to say. I just . . ." Mrs. Jacobs spread her hands briefly to suggest how much all this troubled her.

"Well, I do have something more to say," announced Sue Kramer. Sue was a graduate student at

Barnard, and Charlie had heard she was about to take her doctorate in Sociology. "There are people out there who need to raise forty or fifty dollars a day, every day, to feed their habits, and they get it anywhere and any way they can. And it's going to be like that until those people in Washington work up the guts to legalize heroin."

"They probably have a piece of the business," Charlie said, and Sue Kramer shot him a sharp look before turning to go on, but Morrison jumped up again.

"We're not talking about heroin. What does it matter *what* they're after? We're supposed to be protected. What are the cops for? Why are we paying taxes?"

Charlie glanced at Yeager to see how he would react, and the lieutenant moved his head to the side and smiled faintly, as if responding to a joke he had already heard a dozen times before. Then Dr. Julian was speaking. "Well, we do have the local law on hand, which is rare enough these days, so let's take advantage of the opportunity . . ." Phil Julian paused for emphasis, blandly confident no one would interrupt him. "Lieutenant, one of our neighbors was killed tonight, and killed in a particularly unpleasant way. What do we do about it? More to the point, what do *you* do about it?"

Lieutenant Yeager looked around the room, obviously measuring their mood, before replying. "If it's any help to you, we'll probably catch that pair. The widow gave us a good description, and, however it may look, we do stay on top of the streets."

"So what?" Morrison said aggressively. "What if you do catch them, they'll be right back out again. What about that murder a month ago over on

Ninety-second Street? It turned out to be some punk who was out on bail for another killing. Now I want to know, how many people do these little bastards have to kill before you'll lock them up for more than a few weeks?"

Charlie thought he saw a flash of anger in Lieutenant Yeager's eye, but the detective answered evenly. "I don't run the courts."

And Lynn said, with a sharpness that surprised Charlie, "Then what do you run? Forgive me, but what can we expect from you people?"

Lieutenant Yeager seemed to be gathering his patience, and again he answered in a reasonable voice. "Juvenile crime is up over three hundred percent in the last three years, ma'am. We do what we can with what we're given. You know the city's crying poor and cutting back everywhere."

He went on to say the court system was a mess, hamstrung by the liberal decisions of the higher court and local ethnic politics, and Charlie heard Sue Kramer whisper to one of her friends, "That's where we get the expression *cop*-out."

It was a whisper meant to be heard, and Lieutenant Yeager stopped abruptly. He turned quickly in Sue's direction and asked sharply, "Do you know how those punks got in? I'll tell you, one of you buzzed them in. Or else they walked through the front door after one of you had opened it. Now what do *we* do to stop that?"

Charlie spoke for the first time. "You want us to develop a fortress mentality and regard everything outside as our enemy."

Yeager pointed to Mrs. Jacobs. "She said it—the streets out there are a jungle. We cover what we can, but you have to learn to help yourself."

Fran Jeffries frowned and said, "Like Mr. Wallace?"

Lieutenant Yeager pulled a pamphlet from his inside coat pocket, unfolded it, and held it out where everyone could see it. Charlie saw a drawing of the stock thief in a golf cap and racoon mask, his clenched hand full of stolen jewelry. Bad bureaucratic art with the broadest possible recognition. The title was WHAT CAN *YOU* DO?

"This pamphlet was left in your lobby last month," Lieutenant Yeager said. "I know because I left it there myself, but apparently Mr. Wallace didn't bother to read it." Lieutenant Yeager turned to the first page. "Right here, can everybody see? 'Don't be a hero!' He got killed for a few bucks. Now what do *we* do about that?"

Chambers stood up. He was a soft-spoken and courteous black man, who was an associate professor of Economics over at Columbia. His voice seemed to cool the growing heat in the room. "Are you asking us to organize, Lieutenant?"

"Yes, sir, I am," Yeager said earnestly. "It's worked in other buildings. You need a buddy system, lobby monitors, tenants' committees—we can show you how to set this up."

"And we do your job," Sue Kramer said.

Lieutenant Yeager didn't look at her as he answered, "No matter whose job it is, it's your life."

Lynn stepped out next to Lieutenant Yeager. Her face was flushed and her eyes bright in what Charlie had learned to recognize as her look of purpose. "But we do have to do something, Sue, and maybe organizing is a way to begin." She paused to look around the room. "We all live here together, but I've been here

24

six years and this is the first time some of us have even bothered to speak to each other."

"Oh, it's not that bad, Lynn," Phil Julian said in his cocktail-party drawl, "some of us manage to say good morning now and then. And I've complained about your dog, haven't I, Mr. Morrison?"

Morrison nodded with satisfaction. "Damn lucky I have a dog."

The child in Murphy's arms woke up and began to cry.

The evening ended in a general agreement that they had to do something to secure their common safety, but nothing definite was decided. Lieutenant Yeager left with the promise that he would come back and continue to counsel them, and people left for their own apartments in a subdued mood. Fran Jeffries stayed behind to help pick up the coffee cups. She was a divorced woman in her middle thirties, who usually seemed to be holding to a dry youthfulness. She was always on a diet, always beginning a new exercise program, trying to save something of herself for a man she hadn't yet met. Tonight she looked tired and older, as though she wasn't going to make it after all.

"How's Laurie?" Lynn asked.

Laurie was Fran's five-year-old. "Oh, she's fine," Fran said. "I got her to sleep early. Once she goes down, she's good for the night."

After Fran left, Charlie sent Robbie to bed. He noticed that the kid seemed depressed, so after he finished helping Lynn clean up, he looked in on him. Robbie was sitting on the edge of his bed with his head in his hands.

"Hey," Charlie said softly, "what's the trouble?"

Robbie looked up. His eyes were red. "Nothing, Dad."

"Since when do you cry over nothing?"

Robbie was silent, struggling with whatever was bothering him, and Charlie waited patiently, having learned long ago it was a mistake to push Robbie. Finally, Robbie said, "Those boys who killed that man upstairs ..."

He paused, unable to go on, until Charlie asked, "Yes, what about them?"

Robbie swallowed and looked away. "I think I let them in."

"What do you mean?"

Now Robbie began to cry in earnest. "I think I saw them out in the vestibule. They were looking at the nameplates, and I remember wondering who they could know. They looked mean, so I hurried by them and used my key."

Again he fell silent. Charlie felt a kind of yawning emptiness, and then he thought: Why does this have to touch us? And was instantly ashamed of the thought. It was everyone's problem. He asked Robbie, "Do you think they followed you in?"

"I didn't hear the door close. That was one of the things I used to do when you first gave me the key. I'd see how far up the stairs I could get before I heard the door close, you know, racing myself. It was just a game, and I got tired of it, but I still kind of half listen for the door, and I didn't hear it. That was after practice—"

"Did you hear anything else?"

"No, well ..." Robbie faltered and began to cry in a way Charlie hadn't heard him cry in several years. A palpable weight settled on Charlie's heart.

"Hey, Robbie, Robbie, you don't know for sure, and even if you did—"

Robbie looked him briefly in the eye as he broke in to say, "I looked over the railing, Dad, I saw them."

Charlie took Robbie in his arms. Oh, Jesus, he thought, why couldn't he have kept this off his son? They should have moved up to Nyack. He should have been willing to commute. And it was his fucking vanity again. He hadn't wanted to be stereotyped as a commuter because he had wanted to continue to believe he was an artist, and a metropolitan, proud to live in the greatest urban experiment since Rome. It was so bogus. He tried to say something useful to Robbie, telling him he couldn't be responsible for everything he ever did because you could never be sure how things were going to turn out, some things had to be thought of as accidents, otherwise your burden grew too great to bear, but he always felt like such a fraud when he spoke to his son, so confidently giving Robbie the advice he still found so hard to accept himself.

After Robbie settled down to sleep, Charlie went into his own bedroom, where he found Lynn standing in her underwear in front of a mirror, creaming her face. Their eyes met in the mirror, and she said, "That Phil Julian sounds like an ass."

Lynn's long white legs, easily her best feature, reminded him of how horny he had been earlier. Now he felt nothing, as he said, "Maybe he's so surprised they let him be a doctor and play with people's parts, he still hasn't gotten over it."

Lynn wasn't giving. "I bet he's some doctor."

"As a matter of fact, I've heard he's pretty good."

She was silent for a moment, smoothing her face with both hands. Charlie sat down on the edge of the bed and began to take off his shoes. "Charlie," she went on in a different tone, "do you think we should buy a gun?"

He looked up, shocked. Again their eyes met, and she continued, "I'm serious."

"Baby, a year ago you were collecting signatures on a gun-control petition."

"That was then." She came over and sat down beside him. She took his hand and said earnestly, "I didn't tell you before, but last week someone followed me home."

"What?"

"It was when I went up for the commercial. On the way home this man started following me. And I *knew* it was me he was after, because I saw him leaning against the entrance to the subway, looking the women over as they came out, and I know he decided on me. I could sense it. He pretended he was just going somewhere, but he was always right behind me, and he followed me around two corners, and it was just the most awful feeling. I've never been so scared."

"What did you do?"

"Why, I started to run. I ran the last three blocks in a panic, and then when I got to our door I couldn't find my key and I was just frantic. Fortunately, someone was coming out, so I ran in. I got in here and chained the door, and just stood there shaking. I even had a drink, straight vodka, so you know how upset I was."

He hugged her, feeling her still shuddering slightly with the recollection, and he could think of nothing to say. After a long moment, she continued, "Charlie, do you remember when we lived in the Village, we never even locked our door?"

"That was twelve years ago."

A lot had happened in those twelve years. Among other things, they had had Robbie and had been forced to grow up themselves. He still remembered the first evening when they had realized they were the adults. They had laughed over it. It had seemed silly, because adults were supposed to be the ones who knew what to do.

CHAPTER TWO

A week passed, a week during which it began to feel like summer in the city, when the small trees along the edges of the sidewalks began to leaf out, and window boxes appeared, and the fruit-and-vegetable stands along Broadway began to show fresh greens. The girls were out in blouses and shorts, and the life of the streets was suddenly more interesting to Charlie Hyatt. Most mornings he walked over to the subway station and rode the IRT down to midtown, and in the afternoon he came back the same way, and he always seemed to find something of interest on the streets. New York was such a complex city, so full of such a variety of life, and the contrasts were often startling. The city would always be summed up for Charlie Hyatt in a scene he witnessed during his early days in the Village. He had hoped for the theater then, he had hoped to scale the heights of great art and become the hero of his people, and he'd been out one evening to catch an off-Broadway production over on a side street east of Second Avenue. He barely remembered the play, but he never forgot something he saw just before. Just outside the theater he had watched a couple step from a chauffeured limousine and carefully pick their way around a wino who was sleeping in the gutter.

It was this very compression that made New York so exciting to Charlie Hyatt, and he seldom went on to remember how the wino's ankles, sticking out from the short legs of his cast-off pants, had been circled with a dark pattern of half-healed sores. Now to this ugly image he was forced to add Wallace's face as he had slipped through Charlie's door. But Charlie had an idea that his mind, and perhaps most minds, like the sundial, recorded only clear days. He didn't want to remember, and, in a real sense, he couldn't remember. Who wanted to walk the streets constantly remembering that some awful violence might lie only a heartbeat in the future?

He was forced to realize how swiftly he had smoothed the Wallace killing away when he had a talk with Bill McElroy, the network VP who was in charge of his show. McElroy had slipped into the control booth during the final run-through. Naturally, there was trouble on the set. Lorraine Ryan had flubbed twice, stumbling over the word "quixotic," before she looked up at the booth window to say, "I'm sorry, but I can't get my tongue around that fucking word. And I just don't believe what Richard has got me saying. It's almost painful."

At that moment, Charlie saw McElroy, leaning against the tape console with his arms folded across his chest. Charlie touched a key and said, "All right, Lorraine, try substituting 'impractical' and let's keep it going." There was no further trouble, and when the run-through was finished. McElroy asked him up to the commissary for a cup of coffee before airtime. After an exchange of pleasantries, they were silent until they were seated at one of the yellow plastic tables. Then McElroy asked, "Are you having script problems?"

Charlie wasn't really worried about McElroy. McElroy was a good gray straight shooter who took the trouble to keep up with his shows, and *Under the Same Sky* was holding its own in the middle-afternoon soap ghetto, but no one who worked for the network could ever be entirely secure, because there was an area of network policy that was both mysterious and mercurial. They had canceled even successful shows. They betrayed a chronic appetite for the extraordinary. So he answered with some care. "Sure I'm having script problems. Why should I be unique?"

McElroy smiled. "Too bad we can't steal Latham. She's supposed to be like a machine."

"It's true, she's very good, but you still have to feed money in one end before the scripts come out the other, and that kind of talent doesn't go for scale."

"Yes, yes." McElroy reacted as if a sensitive nerve had been hit.

Charlie went on, "And you know scale, as good as it seemed a few years ago, just hasn't kept pace with inflation, particularly not in this town of all places, and it makes a problem which is probably going to get worse."

"I know. Look, Charlie, I'm your rabbi, and whenever I can get you more money I will. I know you've always respected your budget and I appreciate that. And otherwise, no problems?"

"No, things are going along. I'd still like to work in an incest theme, really laundered—"

"Not yet. Not even soon."

Charlie shrugged and sipped his coffee, noticing how bad it was.

"By the way," McElroy went on, "I heard about the trouble in your building last week."

"Did it make the papers?"

"No, one of your neighbors is my internist. Phil Julian?"

"Yeah, he lives just below us."

"He said you were setting up a tenants' committee."

Charlie looked up, wondering where the other man was heading. "We're going through the motions. Why?"

"Because I've been there. The committees, the meetings with the cops, and it's all a waste of time."

Charlie remembered that McElroy lived about six blocks from him, in a large co-op on West End Avenue.

"Were you having problems too?"

"Sure." McElroy smiled slightly as he paraphrased Charlie's words: "Why should we be different? They weren't quite as bad. No one was killed. But we had a couple of muggings, a rape, and finally it got so bad the junkies were walking off with our television sets and stereos in broad daylight. My kid lost his trumpet, and someone upstairs was taken for a bag of unset diamonds he had bought as a hedge against inflation. They were walking in and out like they lived in the building."

"So what did you do, dig a moat?"

McElroy looked down at his cup, and for the first time he seemed hesitant. "Nope, we hired a security guard."

"You're putting me on."

"Not for a minute. We hired a security guard, and it was the smartest thing we could have done. He's been there a year and there hasn't been a single incident."

"I can't argue with that, but couldn't you have used a doorman instead?"

McElroy shook his head firmly. "We had three in a row. The first two drank, and one of them was hitting on the women in the building, and the third one got beat up so badly he's probably still in the hospital. That's when we hired John Mack, and he's made a job of it. What I was wondering, Charlie, is do you want me to have him give you a call?"

Charlie stared at McElroy, and again the older man looked away. "This John Mack?" Charlie asked, to make sure he had understood.

"Yes, he's our man, and maybe he can give you some useful advice." McElroy met Charlie's gaze again, and his eyes were concerned. "Charlie, I know you well enough to know your liberal sensibilities are cringing, but this is a life-and-death problem, and we need more help than the police can provide. You know, a security guard doesn't bother anyone who's not trying to bother you."

"It isn't that so much, though I admit the idea troubles me, but I just wonder where this city's going. We were raised to believe in progress, and taught to want to contribute to that process. Now look."

"Well," McElroy said, "the crunch is on. We're eating off the top of the cake—think what it's like on the bottom."

"Most people don't care." Charlie glanced at his watch. "Hey, I've got to crack. Thanks for the coffee."

"That's okay."

As Charlie Hyatt left the commissary, he glanced back and saw that McElroy was still sitting where he had left him, holding his cup halfway to his mouth, as if it had been arrested there by the urgency of some thought. Something was bothering McElroy. Charlie picked these things up. He sensed trouble in others and had long ago required himself to realize that he was seldom the cause of it. Who could tell about Bill McElroy? He left a lot unsaid and made his way in a stratum of their ecological system that was filled with exotic predators. Charlie simply hoped McElroy was secure in his own job, because Charlie found him easy to work under. Then he had to put McElroy out of his mind and deal with several lighting problems.

When Charlie mentioned the security guard to Lynn, she frowned. She was scrubbing carrots in the sink, and she paused in her work to ask, "Why do we have to go so far?"

Robbie was practicing in his room, going up and down the scale of thirds, first in one meter, then in another. "I don't know that we do. I'm just telling you what Bill McElroy said."

"I don't like the sound of it."

He smiled as he said, "I'm not surprised. I didn't think you would."

"Well, I don't."

Charlie had often made a joke of saying Lynn was far to the left of Mao Tse-tung. She had been a City

College girl who had filled her life with politically correct causes. She had marched against the war in the sixties, detested Nixon, and written passionately eloquent letters to the *Times*, which they had never printed. She had given money to save the whales, to save the seals and the woodchauffers and the great crested herons. For years she had refused to use paper towels, and the summers they had taken houses on Fire Island or in the mountains she had conscientiously composted their garbage. At parties, Lynn could always be counted on to lead the conversation around to devising ways they might stick it to the great corporations that were systematically undermining the American experiment. "They're creating a new brand of feudalism," she said. "What are the Rockefellers but landed barons, surrounded by faithful serfs?" It sounded smart and it had the smell of truth, and, high on booze and weed, high on youth itself, they had conspired harmlessly like children plotting to expose the hypocrisy of their elders.

But after Charlie had joined the network, no one ever said "sold out," there had been less of this talk, and the paper towels had reappeared in the kitchen because they were "so damn convenient." Still, on large issues they were as firm as ever.

Now, Charlie went on to say, "Still and all, I think we might as well listen to this man. I don't mean to piss on mutual cooperation, but I don't have much faith in the tenants' committee we pulled together."

"But, Charlie, can't you do something?"

"I don't know, Baby. I'm not a leader of men. When we had that meeting Thursday night, all we accomplished was to get drunk drinking beer over at Rosco's. We talked, but talk, to quote someone, is cheap. And speaking of drunk, would you like a drink?"

She was beginning to cut up the carrots. "When I finish with this."

He gave her a quick hug from behind and whispered in her ear. She pushed her bottom up against him and moved it slowly from side to side, as she said, "That's the best proposition I've had all day. As a matter of fact, it's the only one."

He savored the intimacy. "What happened to your flasher?"

"Oh, I'm afraid they locked him up. Poor old thing. That's the police for you. They leave the real monsters loose to prowl and lock up some poor old man who wants you to look at his little purple cock."

"Last time you told me you said it was blue."

She turned to smile over her shoulder. "That was in the winter."

"I guess flashing in the winter is a form of heroism. Maybe even perversion elevated into an art form."

Charlie went into the living room and made himself a tall water and Scotch. He sat down to sip it slowly while he glanced through *Newsweek*. Robbie was now working on something new, something he didn't recognize, and he really listened for a while. The kid could play. Charlie didn't know whether he was pleased or not. Everyone wanted his children to be talented, but talent was a form of slavery, and musical talent so often went begging. In a city of several million there were maybe twenty-five clarinet players who worked full time.

When the phone rang, he automatically said, "I'll get it," and took his drink with him as he went to answer. "Hello," he said, aware that he was making his voice brighter than he really felt.

"Mr. Hyatt?"

"Yes."

"I'm John Mack. Mr. McElroy asked me to give you a call."

"Oh, yes. How are you?"

"Fine. I understand you're having some trouble in your buiding."

"Yes, a man was killed last week by street punks."

"Maybe it would help if I came over and looked around and then had a talk with you."

"Well, I'm just one member of the tenants' committee. I think I'd better talk to the others."

"Where are you located? For my own information I'd like to make a survey."

Charlie hesitated. The voice on the phone was one of those firm official voices that automatically inspire confidence. There was no intimation of hustle in John Mack's approach, only a workman saying if there's a job, let's get at it and get it done.

"I can't speak for the others," Charlie said, "but as far as I'm concerned I think we need some expert help."

"That's what I'm offering."

"Okay, we're over on West Ninety-sixth. Three-oh-four."

"Three-oh-four West Ninety-sixth."

"Right. I'll talk to the others tonight. I'm sure it'll be okay."

"That's fine, Mr. Hyatt, but don't tell anyone I'm going to be making an appraisal, because I want to see how it is under normal conditions. Do you know what I mean?"

"Yes, I think I understand."

"Good. When I get done, I'll give you another call and we can get together and talk."

Charlie could sense the other man getting ready to hang up, and he said quickly, "Wait a minute, what's involved? I mean, do you have a fee for this?"

"No, Mr. McElroy asked me to help you out. That's good enough for me. I'll call you tomorrow or the next day."

"Okay, and thanks."

Charlie replaced the phone, took a pull on his drink, and stared thoughtfully at a Miró reproduction without seeing it. He felt as if he'd just talked to a truant officer or a civil defense warden.

"Who was that?" Lynn called from the kitchen.

"That was Mr. John Mack."

"And who," mimicking his deliberate tone, "is Mr. John Mack?"

"The security guard at McElroy's building."

"Oh." She came into the living room, wiping her hands on her apron. "So what's going to happen?"

"He's going to look the building over for soft spots, and advise us."

Lynn looked skeptical. "Because he's on the side of right."

"Because Bill McElroy asked him to."

"And so he gets his big black shoe in the door."

"Now wait a minute. In the first place, he's got a job. McElroy asked him to help us out, and personally, I'm happy he did. We're amateurs, you know, and this man sounds like a professional."

"Don't you think you should ask Lieutenant Yeager what he thinks?"

"Come on! Yeager's busy shoveling shit every day of the week, and no matter how much trouble we're in, there's always someone who has it worse. Let's hear this man, anyway."

Robbie came down the hall from his room and immediately sensed their tension. He hated for them to fight, and he looked carefully from his mother to his father before he decided nothing serious was going on. Then he asked, "Is dinner ready?"

"No, it isn't," Lynn said.

"Oh, Mom, I'm hungry."

"Why don't you go out for pizza, then?" Lynn said.

"Don't push your mother," Charlie said severely.

Robbie's eyes flashed with anger, but he held his tongue, and went back to his room. "I think I'm ready for that drink," Lynn said.

After dinner, Charlie went out. He knew he shouldn't, it was Tuesday and he still wasn't on top of Thursday's script, but he promised himself he'd get up early and go over it before he left in the morning. He needed to relax and step outside himself for a few hours. It was almost nine o'clock, but the last of the daylight still lingered above the tops of the surrounding buildings, and the streets were alive with anxious traffic. Every third car was a cab.

He walked briskly over to Broadway, crossed with the light, and entered Rosco's. He took a stool at the end of the bar and ordered a Beck's. "How are you tonight?" the bartender, Gabe, asked professionally.

"Just fine," he said, with more heartiness than he felt.

Gabe was a man with an elegant crest of yellow hair and quiet green eyes, and Charlie admired the crisp manner in which he plucked the brown bottle from the cold locker, kicking the thick wooden door closed with his heel as he flicked off the cap, and came walking down the plank, picking up a frosted glass on the way.

"There you are."

Charlie pushed a worn five-dollar bill across the pol-

ished mahogany. He recognized that bartenders employed a form of theater, and many of them had first
come to the city as aspiring actors. Their brisk ballet
was designed to make you forget they were merely
bartenders, and the best of them could even wash
glasses as if it were a vital and essentially masculine
function.

When Gabe brought the change he asked, "Did you
hear they knocked us over last night?"

"No, what happened?"

"Three of them came in around two o'clock. Funny
boys, they were all wearing Halloween masks, three
Darth Vaders, carrying Saturday-night specials, and
they took us for about fifteen hundred, and on the
way out one of them roughed up a girl who was sitting at the bar. They were right off the animal farm."

"Did she do anything?"

Gabe shook his head positively. "Not a thing, she
was just sitting there, probably wishing she was somewhere else, and this creep smashed her, just for
dessert, you know. I mean, I can understand someone
being drove up for cash and just going for it, but this
other stuff, I can't get my mind on it. I know one
thing—they better not drive by for seconds."

He reached under the bar and came up with a
weapon. Charlie had never seen a sawed-off shotgun,
but he knew immediately what it was. Thick, com-
pact, smooth, with the deadly aura of a large poi-
sonous snake. "Isn't that thing illegal?" Charlie asked.

Gabe smiled grimly. "So's robbery."

At this point someone down the bar signaled Gabe,
and he replaced the shotgun and went back to work.
Charlie took a long drink of beer and immediately refilled his glass. It came to him how easily he could
have been sitting at the bar when the gunmen en-

tered. He had been hearing violent stories from his earliest days in New York, but in the last few years there were many more. He stared at the condensation beaded on the side of the brown beer bottle, and the expression "senseless violence" came into his mind. Did that mean there was sensible violence? Wasn't all violence essentially senseless, and wasn't that the very thing? A violent man was like a runaway car that will no longer answer the wheel. Something in the steering mechanism snaps, and brute inertia takes over.

Charlie had two more beers before he decided to go home. He handed Gabe a dollar and received in return the companionable smile reserved for good tippers. He walked along slowly. The sky was dark now, but the streets were as busy as ever. He passed two women whose short, tight skirts and flamboyantly primitive makeup announced their profession to those who were looking. He avoided the question in their eyes, and turned down one of the darker side streets to stitch over one block and down another toward his own door. When the boys approached him, coming down the sidewalk toward him, he automatically measured them and decided they were all right. They wore bright-colored baseball jackets and tight pants, and one was maybe fifteen and the other might have been sixteen. Their heads looked smooth and sleek, like the heads of seals. He automatically adjusted his stride to pass them.

"Hey, mister, you got a buck?"

He paused and looked closer, but saw nothing he hadn't already noticed. Two clean middle-class black kids, trying their luck. He smiled tolerantly, and pulled out the change he'd picked off the bar counter. "How about fifty cents?" he said.

The older one smiled back. "We really need a buck."

"Okay, there you are." He handed a dollar to the older boy. The younger one shifted around, and their attitude changed imperceptibly.

The younger one said, "Hey, what about a buck for me too?"

"Now wait a minute," Charlie said. "You guys asked for a buck, and I gave you one."

"But you got lots. We just saw that."

Charlie started to say, *And I worked for it, too,* but paused, wondering for the moment if these two kids would see what he did as work, rather than an exciting form of adult play. "Look," he said instead, "spread it around. Hit on someone else."

They both backed off, but not retreating. Clearly they were making room to maneuver. The younger one put his hand in the pocket of his baseball jacket; and suddenly something was pointing at Charlie's belly. "What about it?" the younger one asked. "Should we blow him away?"

The older boy, too, put his hand in his pocket, and now both of them were pointing things at him. He couldn't believe what was happening. He didn't believe it. But despite this, the whole core of him turned cold and the beer churned in his stomach.

"Now wait a minute," he began.

The younger boy, clearly the more aggressive, smiled as he said, "I bet he's got more than some shabby buck. I bet he's got a big fat ten spot. How about that? What you got in your pocket anyway?"

If someone wanted to scare you with a gun, they'd be sure to show it to you, if only for a moment. That was the sense of this situation. But you could never be sure. "Leave me alone," Charlie said, and was humiliated to hear the whisper of a whine in his voice. He pulled out another dollar and handed it over. "Now that's all."

"I still think we ought to blow him away." The younger boy was watching his face alertly, sensing his fear and feeling powerful over frightening someone. Suddenly, the two boys turned and ran across the street. Above the slap of their feet, he heard them laughing.

"You couldn't blow your nose," he shouted after them. "I know you don't have guns."

One of them spun around and, fanning his thumb, called, "Bang! Bang!" Then laughed again.

Charlie stood where they left him, feeling drained and empty. Then he shrugged, and smiled at his own confusion. The little punks had hustled him like a fish.

Back home, for reasons he didn't entirely sort out, he decided not to tell Lynn about the incident. Nor did he tell her about the robbery at Rosco's. She was worried enough. He found her in bed, propped on both their pillows, reading a magazine. The blanket was pulled tight beneath her arms, but he saw at a glance she was naked under the covers. This was the signal he'd been waiting for, but he noted it with less interest than he had expected to feel. She smiled as he walked past her toward the bathroom, and asked, "Did you have a good time?"

He shrugged and paused with his hand on the door. "I always think something's going to happen out there, but it almost never does. People who sit in bars are people who want to be at a party all the time."

"Well, you said it."

"I know."

He pissed, brushed his teeth, and then undressed quickly, leaving his shorts on. He barely glanced at his face in the mirror. Tonight there might be something in his eyes he didn't want to see.

CHAPTER THREE

Robbie Hyatt was the first one in the building to see John Mack, though Robbie didn't realize it at the time. He was hurrying home from school because he was due at Jonathon Silverman's tenth-birthday party, and Jonathon had made broad hints how his father had scored a first-run movie to show them. He ran the last three blocks because he was trying to build up his wind for sostenuto passages, and he came tearing into the vestibule, digging his keys out of his jacket pocket, and almost bumped into a man who was bent over studying the nameplates.

He was large, not so much tall as just plain big,

dressed in a plain gray suit, almost exactly the same color as his hat. He straightened up and looked at Robbie, and Robbie saw a broad white face and pale blue eyes. Watchful eyes. Robbie knew many city types, and this man didn't fit. He had more the look of the kind of men they sometimes dealt with when they vacationed in the mountains, and there was something about him that made Robbie faintly apprehensive.

Robbie's apprehension wasn't helped when he opened the door and the man made it clear he intended to follow Robbie inside. Robbie forced himself to ask, "You don't live here, do you?"

"No."

"I'm not supposed to let in anyone I don't know."

Surprisingly, the man smiled. "Good boy. What's your name?"

"Robbie. Robbie Hyatt."

"You look like you're built about right for a shortstop. How about it? Is that your position?"

Robbie shrugged, eager to be upstairs. "I don't play that much ball."

"You don't?"

"I'm in the band."

"Oh. Well, you're right not to let me in, Robbie, but let me just show you a little something. You go in, close the door, and then just wait a moment. Go ahead."

Puzzled, Robbie did as he was told. He stood watching as the door closed and clicked shut. The man did something, and pushed the door open. He stepped in smiling, holding something hidden in his hand.

"You had a key," Robbie said accusingly.

"Nope." He opened his hand to show a plastic credit card. "But this works just as well."

"I've seen that on television, but I didn't think it really worked."

"It shouldn't, Robbie, it shouldn't, but the doors get worn and loose on these old buildings, and anyone can get in. I'll show you how if you like."

"I'm sorry, but I'm in a hurry."

"All right, you go on, and don't worry about me. I'm here to help."

Robbie ran upstairs and let himself into the apartmet. His mother called from the kitchen, "Is that you, Robbie?"

"Yeah. Mom. I've got to change and get over to Jonathon's."

"Will you be home for dinner?"

"Probably. I'll call if I'm going to be late. Hey, Mom, there's some dude poking around downstairs."

Lynn Hyatt came out of the kitchen and followed Robbie down to his room. "What do you mean? Who is it?"

"Just some man. He seems all right."

"Robbie! What's he doing?"

"He said he was here to help."

"Help? What do you mean?"

"Mom, take it easy. I'm sure he's all right."

Lynn's mouth tightened. "Robbie, will you slow down and tell me what's happening?"

They gathered at Rosco's to take John Mack's report, Charlie, Julian, and Chambers, and Charlie also sensed the rural quality in this large quiet man. There was something of the country lawman, a steady sense of competence that was reassuring. They sat around over beers, and John Mack did most of the talking.

He was direct and he looked at each of them in turn, fixing them with his stern blue eyes, and he came off like a forest ranger lecturing them on the danger of careless fires.

"There's no point trying to soften it for you," Mack said. "Your security's a joke. The building's an open invitation to anyone looking for a soft touch."

Charlie caught Dr. Julian's eye, and Julian shrugged. Chambers asked quietly, "What can be done, if anything?" He stared at John Mack, his head cocked, smooth, neat, and brown. Mack took a small sip of his beer.

"A great deal can be done," he said firmly. Mack turned to Charlie. "I think I can outline a program that would close most of the holes, if not all of them."

Charlie nodded. "Yes?"

Mack went on, "You men do represent the tenants in the building?"

"More or less," Dr. Julian said. "We were drafted."

Mack put his large white hands on the table, fingers spread. "Are they ready to make a commitment? There's nothing I can do unless I have full cooperation."

"Wait a minute, Mr. Mack," Charlie said, "I'm a little confused. I thought you were here to give us advice, but you're beginning to sound as if you want this job yourself."

Mack nodded firmly. "Yes, sir, I do."

"But aren't you already employed? Bill McElroy told me you look after his building."

Charlie watched John Mack take another sip of his beer, an even smaller sip than before. Charlie was puzzled and faintly uneasy. Still, he found time to note how large and competent Mack's hands were. Mack replaced his glass on the tabletop, as if it were something he wanted to do just right, and without looking up he asked, "How much do you gentlemen know about me?"

"Nothing, really," Charlie said.

Mack looked up. "So we start even, don't we? Let me tell you something about myself. I was a career soldier. I did twenty years in the army, and when I was discharged I was master sergeant of a rifle company. Yes, I served in Nam. I'm not political, you see? They told me to go fight, and that's what I did. You might say I got used to the action. Not war. I'm not a war lover. But I do like a challenge. I think you men find that in your work. I like it in mine."

Chambers took it up. "And your present job doesn't challenge you?"

"No, sir, that building's been clean for a year now. There's not much for me to do."

"Yes, but if you leave," Charlie objected, "won't the building fall apart again?"

Mack shook his head. "Not at all. You see, the system's operational now, and anyone can run it. That's what I like to do, devise a security system that can almost function by itself. That's the challenge I was talking about." He paused and took a manila envelope from his inside coat pocket. He placed it in the middle of the table. "These are my references. Any questions you might have, you'll find the answers in here. I'm fully bonded, and I'm licensed to carry a sidearm."

There was a silence. Charlie understood its nature. None of them felt like assuming the authority to respond to this unexpected development. Before the silence became awkward, John Mack broke it himself. "Would you gentlemen like me to go up to the bar while you talk this over?"

Dr. Julian waved his slender hands. "That's not

necessary. Let's just say you've given us something to think about."

John Mack went on, "If I can make a suggestion. You see, I've been through this before, and I've found that the best course is to call a meeting of all the tenants. Let me talk to them. I'll point out the flaws in your security and explain how I'd correct them. I'll tell everyone what they can expect from me, and what I'd expect from them. Then they can decide by a simple vote, with no obligation on either side."

"That sounds fair," Charlie said.

"What about money?" Chambers asked.

"We can hammer that out, if the tenants decide they want my services."

John Mack took his hat from the chair beside him. "Now, gentlemen, I'll leave you. If you want to proceed, just give me a call."

He stood and carefully shook hands, briefly and firmly, all around, and walked out.

After a moment, Julian said, "He's something out of the past, isn't he?"

Chambers looked dubious. "I'll tell you the truth, I think he's a racist."

There was another silence, and Chambers smiled and continued, "Yes, I know, you think I see prejudice everywhere, but we develop special instincts, and I made him uncomfortable. He hardly looked at me."

"Does that rule him out?" Charlie asked.

"Not by me," Chambers said. "Half the cops in this city are the same way. I still accept their protection."

"He seems very competent," Charlie said.

"Yes," Julian added, "and that's the point, isn't it? We've become so fucking civilized we can't even protect ourselves. We're too busy. So we hire someone who still has the instincts we've lost."

It seemed to Charlie that Julian had hit the point, and he was faintly surprised to be glimpsing another man beneath the languid socialite physician Julian usually projected. He drained his glass, and asked, "Does anyone besides me want another?"

Chambers shook his head and drew his glass back, but Julian said, "Sure, why not? Hippocrates recommended it, and so did St. Paul, so we have both secular and sacred authority."

"Then we'll drink to them both," Charlie said, with a thrust of gaiety he recognized as the first stages of drunkenness. A little easy, old chum, he thought, even as he was getting up to head for the bar. Gabe was on duty again. He was dressed in leather, like a mountain man, and his vivid yellow hair was carefully styled.

"How you doing?" he asked Charlie, automatically turning on his cool professional smile.

"Well, the woods are burning," Charlie announced cheerfully, "but that's not too bad, because the water's also rising."

"Yeah?" Gabe assessed Charlie's wit and awarded it another smile, before he asked, "What'll you have?"

"Two more beers and two Wild Turkeys."

Charlie hadn't known he was going to order the Wild Turkey until he heard himself asking for it. Well, what the hell, he thought. He questioned his drinking in the morning, not at night. Julian seemed pleased with the whiskey, and he sipped it slowly. Charlie realized the three of them didn't know each other very well. Still, he wanted to talk, so he went back to their original subject.

"Did you smell a faint hint of hustle on that fellow?" he asked.

"No," Chambers said, "just prejudice."

"I thought he was pretty straight," Julian added. "I suppose I think he's the kind of man I should admire. You know, when I was in medical school I thought I wanted to be a general practitioner." He smiled wryly. "I suppose I harbored a fantasy where I would become the beloved doctor of some small town. I'd deliver the babies of the babies I had delivered. It did seem like a useful life. But I meet some of those men at conventions, small-town docs, and they seem dull and embittered, mediocre doctors at best."

Charlie had been hearing this kind of talk since the middle sixties, and he hadn't listened to it then and he didn't intend to listen to it now. "We all suffer from that phony rural sentimentality," he said.

"I think it's real enough," Chambers disagreed. "A hundred years ago most of our parents were working on farms." He smiled subtly. "In one capacity or another."

"I still think it's bullshit," Charlie said. "There's everything you could imagine right in this city."

"Well, that's certainly true," Chambers said dryly.

They all laughed. Charlie's glass was empty, so he got up to get another drink.

CHAPTER FOUR

John Mack delivered his security lecture at night so everyone could hear it, and most of the building turned out. He opened the front door with his Master Charge card, then held it up so all could see. "They told me I could get anything I wanted with this card," he said. "But I'm sure this isn't what they had in mind."

There was a murmur of nervous laughter. Mack looked straight at Charlie as he went on. "So you're wide open here. Well, that's not hard to fix. But control of keys is harder to manage. How many of you have had duplicates made?"

A number of hands went up.

"I thought so. It's the same way in every building. You make a dupe for the guy who delivers the papers and the kid from the supermarket. There are keys all over the neighborhood. So the first thing we do is change the lock and cancel all deliveries—"

Morrison interrupted, "That's inconvenient."

Mack shook his head, and his hard white face firmed. "So's getting robbed. So's getting killed. Is there a Mrs. Jacobs here?"

Mrs. Jacobs looked startled and reached for her husband's arm. "Yes, I'm Mrs. Jacobs."

"No offense, ma-am, but I got in here about an hour ago by ringing your bell."

"Was that you? I thought it was a friend."

"You didn't check, ma'am. I'm not being critical. I'm sure a lot of your neighbors do the same thing. Now, we have to think about mirrors. You need mirrors here, and in front of the elevator—"

"Wait a minute," Charlie said, stepping forward. "The call system doesn't work half the time. We've no way of knowing who's buzzing."

"Okay," Mack said, "then you have to tear out the rest of the system. Eliminate it so no one can buzz the door open. You want to let someone in, walk down and see who it is."

"Come on," Morrison said, "you want us to live in a jail."

Dr. Julian spoke for the first time. "That doesn't seem all that bad."

"Well, sure," Morrison returned, "you live on the first floor. I'm on the fifth."

"I think it's reasonable," Fran Jeffries said. "I'm alone, you know, except for Laurie." She smoothed her daughter's hair. "And I haven't had an easy night since it happened."

"Exactly, ma'am," Mack said. "We're talking about a serious situation. You got a floating junkie population out here on the streets and they need a fix every day. That's a fact you got to live with. It isn't *going* to go away. It's a big business, and it's only going to get worse."

"All right," Charlie said, "most people are already frightened enough. Let's say we make these changes, what would your function be?"

John Mack was ready for the question. "I'd keep this place secure," he told Charlie, then looked around at the others. "I'd baby-sit you for a while, particularly during high-risk times. I'd be here at night and sometimes during the day. I'd always be available in case of an emergency."

Charlie heard Julian asking, "I assume you have a home?"

"Yes, sir," Mack answered easily. "In Queens. But I'm not married, so I don't have to report to any one. For the first few months I'd be around here like a bad smell. Those junkies out there on the street will know I'm here. You can depend on that."

"Excuse me," said Mrs. Jacobs. "You said there couldn't be any more deliveries, but I don't get up and down stairs too well anymore, and I was wondering—"

Mack broke in. "What's your first name, ma'am?"

"Why, it's Ida."

"Well, Ida, don't you worry about your groceries, I'll see that you get them."

After Mack was gone, the committee and the others who were interested met in the Hyatts' apartment.

Lynn immediately began to make coffee, and Charlie paused in the kitchen to ask her, "Well, what do you think of him?"

Lynn set the filter in the Chemex before she answered, "I don't know. You're right, he seems competent. I just hate the idea."

"Well, I don't love it."

Charlie went into the living room, where he found Chambers and Julian already sitting at the dinner table, their faces oddly shaded in the glow of the Tiffany lamp. Fran Jeffries was sitting on the couch, Laurie in her lap. Morrison sat across from her. Chambers was running some figures on a pocket calculator.

Charlie sat down next to Fran and reached over to tousle Laurie's hair. Seeing Laurie reminded him of when Robbie had been younger. He sometimes missed all the younger Robbies. The baby who had smiled secretly, hour after hour. The toddler who had taken his first steps to dive into Charlie's arms, smiling as if he knew perfectly well what he had just done.

Fran looked tired, and when she thought no one was watching, her face grew tense and unhappy. "How are you?" Charlie asked, making his tone say he really wanted to know. Fran stared at him for a moment. She had nice eyes. Direct and sensitive.

"I guess I'm having a few bad days. Sometimes it seems like I'm just hanging on and only getting from one day to the next."

"I'm sorry," Charlie said. "Can we help?"

"Oh, no, I don't need anything where I can just say *this* is what I need. Do you know what I mean?"

"I think so."

"Alimony and child support can become a kind of

cage, you know, a cage you sit in while waiting for your life to begin again, only it can't because you can't get out, and nothing can get in."

Charlie was spared trying to answer because at that moment Chambers announced, "It comes to thirty-three thirty a month?"

"A unit?" Charlie asked.

"Yep!" Chambers answered, smiling ruefully.

"Shit," Morrison said, clearly disgusted. "And on top of that this asshole wants us to run up and down stairs four or five times a day. Jesus."

"I'm for it," Julian said. "It's worth it to know we're safe."

"But will we really know that?" Charlie asked. "Is anyone ever safe?"

Morrison made an impolite noise, and Julian laughed. Chambers said, "I'm for it. It's only eight dollars a week. Some of you spend more than that on croissants and tennis lessons."

"Crescent rolls," Charlie said. "Why won't anyone say crescent rolls?"

"I'll pay gladly," Fran said. "And if anyone can't contribute, I mean, if they should have financial problems, the rest of us can make up the difference."

"That's called socialism, Fran," Chambers said.

"I don't care what it's called," Fran said spiritedly, "if it gives me a feeling of security in my own home."

"How about you, Charlie?" Chambers asked. "Are you going along?"

Lynn came through the door with the coffee cups, so Charlie put it to her. "How about it, Lynn, are we going along?"

She frowned as she said, "I guess we are."

Morrison stood up, rubbing his elbows. "All right, I'm going to pass on the coffee. I've got to walk my dog before the muggers come out for the night. I'll say this much now. You'll have to have the whole building vote. I'll go along with the majority."

When Morrison was gone, Julian said quietly, "There's a strange man."

Charlie smiled as he added, "I wonder how we look to him."

Fran said she had to leave also, it was Laurie's bedtime, and as she stood to go, Charlie automatically noted how good her body was. She worked on it, and it showed. Here was a mine that shouldn't be idle, he thought, and then went on to hope something lucky would happen to her.

He sat with Lynn, and they talked to Julian and Chambers. They were amusing men, and he was beginning to enjoy them. They talked about the city, about the dogshit in the streets and how the park was becoming a swamp and how the mayor never did anything. "That poor bastard," Charlie said. "He's got the worst job since captain of the *Titanic*." He went on to ask if anyone wanted his coffee braced, but they all said no, and he was able to prevent himself from drinking alone.

After they left, Charlie went in to see if Robbie was in bed. He was under the covers, reading

"What's that?" Charlie asked.

Robbie shrugged one shoulder. "Just a book I got from the school library."

"I can see that. What's it called?"

"Tom Swift and His Giant Robot."

Charlie smiled with pleasure as he said, "I used to read those things." He went on to point at the large poster of Kiss tacked over the desk. "But I never had anything quite like that on my wall."

"What did you have, Dad?"

He continued smiling as he tried to remember. "Oh, I don't know. Charts of the geologic ages, that sort of thing. I used to make model airplanes, and I had a couple of them hung from the ceiling with thread."

"That sounds neat," Robbie said.

"Yes, I thought I wanted to be an airline pilot."

"Wouldn't it be great if you were? You could bring back stuff from all over, and Mom and I could fly around for nothing."

"Ah! No one flies around for nothing, Robbie." He stood up. "Don't read too late."

He found Lynn getting ready for bed. On impulse he asked her, "How'd you like a fast fuck?"

"I don't know, why don't you try it and see what happens?"

Afterward she said, "I was too tired. The silly thing is that almost every afternoon around four I get so horny I can hardly stand it, and you're never here."

"We need a vacation," he said. "Let's start thinking about how to get away."

"I thought we were going to buy a co-op?"

"We have to live, baby," he said.

She was silent for a while. Then she went on, "I have a bad feeling about this place now. I really would like to get out. I keep waiting for the other shoe to drop."

Charlie was at the T.V. studio when it happened, but Lynn told him about it, and then he heard Fran's story. He could imagine the whole thing just as if he had been there.

Fran and Lynn had both been in the basement laundry room. Lynn was just finishing up their wash when Fran came in. Laurie was with her. "Well, we meet at the riverbank again," Fran said.

It was a joke they had made before, and Lynn went on, "Beating clothes on a flat rock might be an improvement over these machines."

"It might at that." Fran indicated one of the washers. "Did they fix this one yet?"

"I don't know. Do what I do, put in your quarter and then pray." She smiled at the little girl. "How are you, Laurie?"

"'Kay," Laurie said. "See my Superstar Barbie."

Lynn studied the impossibly slender girl doll. "She's beautiful."

"Yes, and she's fashion," Laurie confided.

Lynn left at that point, and she knew nothing more until an hour later, when Fran appeared at her door, her clothes torn and the side of her face puffed and angry with the beginning of a massive bruise. Fran told the story then and told it again and again in the weeks that followed, as if the retelling were a rite of exorcism she compulsively followed.

When Lynn left the laundry room, Fran began to sort her clothes—delicates in one pile, the heavier things in another, hoping to work it all into two loads—while Laurie sat quietly in one of the old chairs, dressing and redressing her doll. She always made a point of saying that Laurie had just asked her if she'd wash Barbie's evening gown. Then Laurie said, "Hello," to someone.

Laurie was a friendly child, and Fran straightened up and turned expecting to see one of her neighbors. Instead, she saw a large black man. He was extravagantly dressed in tight bellbottoms and a red double-breasted coat with peaked lapels. His collar was open, and there was a glint of something gold among the tightly wound hairs on his chest. His head was shaved, and he wore wraparound sunglasses. He stood, almost filling the doorway, looking around carefully. When he saw Fran's purse where she had left it on the dryers, he started toward it.

"You can have it," Fran said.

"Why thank you, mama," he said, in a surprisingly high voice.

There was a nasty suppressed sarcasm in his tone that added to Fran's fear. While he was shucking out her purse, she grabbed up Laurie and ran for the door. He caught her before she took three steps.

"I'll scream," she said. "The super's apartment's right down the hall."

She felt his large hand close over her mouth.

"You shut the fuck up!"

Laurie began to cry.

"All right, little girl, it's all right," he said. Then he whispered in Fran's ear, "You jes' keep it shut, you don't want your little girl's face cut up."

Fran felt strangely clearheaded, and everything happened as if it were in slow motion. The man threw her down on her own laundry, and held her there with one hand between her breasts while with the other he pulled down her slacks and pants. All in one motion, like a bear ripping something off a shelf. *Jesus,* she thought. *Jesus.* He forced her legs apart with his body. She heard Laurie say, "Don't hurt my mommy!" He was surprisingly small, and she was more aware of his heavy hands on her arms and his breath beating against her ear than she was of his cock. He struggled on her, saying, "You bitch, you dirty bitch." Then he was standing up, staring down at her. His sunglasses were tilted, giving him a crazy look. Just go, she thought. Then she saw him move, and something exploded in her head. It wasn't until she came to that she realized he had kicked her in the face.

She stood up immediately. The man was gone. Laurie was standing there sobbing. Fran pulled up her slacks, grabbed her purse and Laurie, and ran upstairs to Lynn's apartment. She pushed Laurie at Lynn and said, "Watch her for a moment." Then she ran upstairs to her own apartment, where she immediately douched. Only when this was finished did she begin to cry.

CHAPTER FIVE

John Mack went to work in the building the day after Fran was raped. The tenant vote was 23 units for to only 3 against, and two of the holdouts came over when they saw the size of the majority. The remaining holdout was Sue Kramer, the graduate student, who lived on the fifth floor. "Even rapists don't like to walk up four flights," she said airily. "And I'm not going to have some asshole telling me who I can give my key to."

It was left to Charlie to call Mack and tell him what they had decided. He reached Mack in his Queens apartment, and Mack said he could start right away. "Don't you have to give notice over at McElroy's?" Charlie asked.

"I already did."

Charlie was startled. "Were you that sure of us?"

"No, I knew you needed me, but I wasn't counting on you. To tell you the truth, I got the word that one of the deputy mayors was moving in, and that means a twenty-four-hour police guard on the building. So I was finished there in more ways than one."

"Well," Charlie said cheerfully, "we're glad to get you, and it's good to know those people are going to be protected as well."

Mack wasted no time. In a few days he had the lock changed, the door squared, and the hall lined with strategically placed mirrors. The round gray eye of a television camera watched over the lobby, and John Mack could monitor all activity from the basement room he had set up as his headquarters. The next time Charlie ran into McElroy in the hallway, he stopped him to say how much they all appreciated John Mack, how much more secure they felt.

McElroy nodded. "That's good to hear."

"I'm glad we didn't steal him from you."

"Oh, no, that's okay."

"Look, now that you've got a deputy mayor for one of your neighbors—"

Charlie had been going to make some joke about getting his parking tickets squared, but at that moment another VP came up and said, "Bill I have to talk to you right now." Charlie excused himself and walked away, wondering at the puzzled look he had seen so briefly on McElroy's face. Then he forgot the incident.

That night Phil Julian knocked on their door to invite them down for a drink. Charlie was glad to go, and Lynn seemed interested. Charlie guessed that she wanted to see how the Julians had decorated their apartment. It was severe modern. Hard-lined furniture, largely black and white, kinetic sculpture, and geometric paintings. Every detail carefully chosen. Claire Julian, a slender woman with prematurely iron-gray hair, was as carefully detailed herself.

On a Lucite coffee table, through which they could see the white shag rug, was a model of a beach house. As he was getting their drinks, Julian explained that this was the house they were building in the Hamptons. "It was supposed to be finished by the end of May. Now it's June, and with any luck I suppose we can actually be in it for the Labor Day weekend."

Big bucks, Charlie thought, not without some envy.

"It's lovely," Lynn said politely. "What part of the Hamptons?"

"East," Claire said, "on the beach at Amagansett. We'll have to have you out."

"If it ever gets done," Julian said, handing Charlie a large Scotch. "We've got a gay architect and a Mafia builder. How's that for soap opera?"

"Sounds more interesting then the one I'm doing." Charlie said.

The bell rang, and Claire crossed to the foyer. She was back in a moment with John Mack following her. Mack wore the same gray suit he always wore, and he was carrying a clipboard and a large manila envelope.

"Mr. Mack," Julian said with a faintly ironic courtesy. "Would you like a drink?"

Mack looked around the apartment as he shook his head. "No thank you, sir. I just come to bring you your new keys for the front door."

Mack opened the manila envelope and brought out

two keys, handing one to Julian and the other to Claire. He nodded at Charlie and said, "I can give you yours now, and save myself a trip." He brought out two more keys.

"We'll need three," Charlie said. "Our son carries his own."

"Is that smart?" Mack asked.

"He's had his own key since he turned ten. It means a lot to him, and he's careful."

Charlie was aware that he was making too much of this, because he was remembering Robbie's tearful confession the night of the murder.

"Okay," Mack said. "But warn him to be extra careful. Now if I can just get you to sign." He handed the clipboard and a pen to Charlie, who found his name in the neatly printed list. He signed and passed the board on to Lynn.

"Isn't this all pretty elaborate?" Julian said. "I feel like we were being issued code books."

"Believe me, Doctor, it's necessary. I can't tell you how important it is not to have duplicate keys floating around."

"You know, John," Claire Julian said, "we have a maid—"

"Please let her in yourself, ma'am, or else make arrangements with me and I'll take care of it. I'm sure she's trustworthy, but you never know who she might come in contact with. I mean, say she has a boyfriend who does a little hustling on the side."

"She's fifty-five, married with six children."

"But you just can't tell. Better to be safe than sorry. And if anyone *loses* a key, please let me know at once."

Julian looked up from signing the clipboard. "Oh, you'll be the first to know, John."

"And, Doctor, when you get a few minutes, maybe one night this week, I'd like to talk to you."

Julian sighed and passed the clipboard to his wife. "What's on your mind, John?"

"Security, sir. You're the only ground-floor apartment, and you have to be extra careful."

"I don't know how we could be any more careful," Julian said, letting his growing exasperation show.

"Your living-room windows overlook the street and they're okay. But your kitchen windows are right on the alley."

"John, those windows are barred."

"With licorice, Doctor."

"What are you saying?"

"I think there are some more precautions you could take."

"I don't."

Charlie saw Mack's look of patient respect slip a little as he said, "Beg pardon?"

Julian went on in his ironical manner, "John, I know you're trying to do your job. You're very conscientious, and I respect that. But this is not a military fort. Okay?"

"In a manner of speaking, it is, sir."

"Well, if the Indians attack, I'll send up a fast flare."

Mack was silent for a moment, absorbing the sarcasm. Then he nodded and said, "Good enough, sir, if you say so." He took the clipboard from Claire. "I'd better hand out the rest of these keys." Claire moved to open the door for him, but he went on, "That's all right, Mrs. Julian. I can let myself out."

After Mack was gone, Julian looked around and smiled as he said, "When do you think he'll start stringing up the barbwire?"

"It *is* annoying," Claire added. "Do I have to get his clearance every time Mildred comes in to clean?"

"Hey," Charlie said, "wait a minute. This is what we're paying him for, remember? The good old days—and how good were they?—seem to be gone bye-bye."

Julian smiled. "We know that, Charlie, we're just exercising the prisoner's inalienable right to bitch."

"He does look a little like a guard, doesn't he," Charlie added, laughing at the thought.

"Yes," Julian agreed. "Barton McLane."

"And who's Barton McLane?" Lynn wanted to know.

"Ah!" Julian said. "To be that young."

When they were getting ready for bed, Charlie asked Lynn, "Well, what did you think of it?"

Lynn was brushing her hair. "Think of what?"

"The Julians' apartment."

"You're such a smartass," she said with a smile. "You know what I thought."

"It would be like living in a lab, wouldn't it? All that stainless steel next to all that white."

Lynn laughed, and that pleased Charlie. She didn't always laugh at his jokes. He went on, "You could say it's a nice place to visit but I wouldn't want to live there."

She put down her hairbrush and gave her face a close inspection, like a curator looking over a painting for signs of deterioration. "You're in a good mood," she said.

"I suppose. I can't be depressed all the time. I'm going to give Robbie his key in case he gets out of here before either of us is up."

"Don't wake him."

"I won't."

Robbie was sleeping on his back, with one hand against his cheek and the other across his chest. His reading light was on, and his book lay beside his bed. Charlie found the boy's key ring in the pants he had taken off, and added the new door key. Then he turned off the light and went back to his own bedroom.

It became one of those nights he couldn't sleep. Charlie hated them. After an hour of switching from one position to another and turning his pillow to bring up the cool underside, he got up and took a couple of slugs straight from the bottle. But rather than calm him, the liquor was stimulating. Shit, he thought, if he couldn't sleep, why should he be miserable as well? He dressed and went out, telling himself he'd be back in an hour.

He walked briskly, alone on the streets. Fletch had closed his newsstand and gone home. The mom-and-pop superette was also closed and barred. But Broadway still streamed cabs, and the sign in front of Rosco's was lit. He cut across with the light, and on the far corner he saw John Mack. Mack wasn't alone. He was talking to a large black man, one of those who shaved their heads, hoping someone would take them for Issac Hayes, or Big Julie Johnson. As Charlie came closer, he saw Mack hand the man something.

As Charlie passed them, Mack put his hand to the brim of his hat, in a casual salute, and said, "Hello, Mr. Hyatt. You're out late."

"Can't sleep."

The black man stood silently, his shades as blank as the eyeholes of a gas mask.

"That can be a problem," Mack said.

"It happens sometimes," Charlie said, going on.

Rosco's was nearly empty. Two men and the bartender were watching Johnny Carson. Charlie joined them, drinking bourbon with a beer wash. Later, when he was back in bed, still unable to sleep, Charlie began to consider how odd it had been to find John Mack out on Broadway late at night, talking with street characters. Then he realized that the black man answered the description of the rapist who had grabbed Fran Jeffries in the laundry room and screwed her right in front of her kid.

For a moment the idea buzzed in his mind. Then he told himself that was how innocent men ended up in prison.

CHAPTER SIX

It was Saturday afternoon, and Robbie was getting a haircut, an ordeal he always put off as long as he could, until his mother insisted. At first she made lame jokes, saying if he didn't get a haircut she'd have to get him a dog license, or switch him from clarinet to violin, which he didn't understand, and when he complained to his father that all the kids wore their hair long, his father would say, "Style is a tyrant," which was something else he wasn't sure he understood. Finally, they ended by insisting, and threatening his allowance and his privileges, and he would have to go down to Max Steiner's shop and surrender.

Old Steiner was a minor neighborhood curiosity because he had a number tattooed on his forearm. The Nazis had marked him when they put him in their concentration camp. Robbie had been told not to stare at the number, and he tried not to, but whenever he saw the number it caught his eye like something shameful, like the yellowish stain he had once glimpsed in the crotch of Margot Herzog's underpants.

Any haircut from Steiner was a form of war. Steiner, who had probably learned barbering in the concentration camp, tried to cut off as much hair as he could, and Robbie was determined to lose as little as possible, and get out of the chair as fast as he could. He had developed many strategies, such as claiming he had suddenly fallen sick, or had to take a leak.

This morning he saw John Mack through the front window and, improvising, told Steiner he had to see Mack with a message from his father.

"Now you sit a minute. If I don't get the hair off your ears, your mother come to give me hell."

"I'll come back. I gotta see him. Really!"

He slid out of the chair, taking off the apron. Steiner spread his hands and asked the ceiling, "What am I supposed to do? I try to cut decent."

While Robbie rooted in his pocket for the haircut money, Steiner shook his head and said, "I guess you're too old for a lolly, aren't you?" Which Robbie knew meant he expected to be tipped. The old fraud. He paid up, and ran out onto the street. Mack was gone, but in a moment he saw him down the street, standing on the corner, glancing around. Mack had the look of a man up to something interesting, and since Robbie had nothing to do, he decided to follow him.

The afternoon was warm and the sky, above the buildings, was a cloudless blue. The street people were out and mixing with the crowds of shoppers. Robbie had been studying street types for years, and he was an eager connoisseur of the tough-dude style—the essence of which was anti-style, to be as down and raunchy as possible. Tough dudes rejected neatness and safety, they scorned good looks, and their appearance was designed to suggest that they were mean and dangerous. They wore heavy boots, thick belts, and expressions of studied indifference.

Ahead of him, Robbie saw Mack crossing the street, moving with the casual power of a large bear. He seemed to be following a black man, who was drifting along the street on his own errand. The black man followed another street style: hte superfly-pimp. He wore a large fuzzy white fedora and a belted light-tan overcoat. His zippered cordovan boots were polished to a high gloss, and he moved through the Saturday crowds like a noble at a village fair. He seemed unaware of Mack just behind him.

Robbie cut across the street, bluffing two cars, sprinting around a Checker cab, round and fat as a pregnant yellow cow, and reached the other side just in time to see Mack following the black dude into a doorway. When he reached the door, Robbie saw narrow wooden steps leading up. He hesitated; then curiosity pushed him forward. He climbed the steps, to come out in a ping-pong palace. Only two of the ten large green tables were in action. Two soldiers, their battle jackets off, were bent into a savage volley, and in another corner a Puerto Rican was teaching his girl the game. At the far end of the loft, an old man sat behind a counter, reading a newspaper.

Robbie saw Mack going along a corridor that led to

the toilets. He hesitated, but again curiosity pushed him. His dad had told him he could trust Mack, so he wasn't afraid. He walked slowly down to the door of the men's room, getting the rank smell of urine while he was still in the hallway. He heard an explosive scuffle and a high-pitched voice shouting: "Hey, man, *who* the fuck are you!" The door was partly open, and just inside, in the greenish half light, he saw Mack handling the superfly black as easily as he might have handled a kid. Yanking one arm up the middle of his back until the dude screamed, and holding him there while he went through his pockets. Mack found something, and let the man go.

"That cost *money!*" the dude said.

"No kidding?" Mack said in a soft, almost disinterested tone. "Well, then, maybe you'll remember what I told you. Now get out of here."

Robbie shrank aside to let the black man pass. The man paused in the doorway to yell at Mack, "I'll get you, turkey!"

Mack didn't bother to answer.

The man swore again and started out. Robbie heard his boots on the wooden floor. Then he heard something that astonished him. "Come on in, Robbie," John Mack said.

Suddenly Robbie felt foolish, and more than a little frightened. What he had just seen was new to him. He had watched a hundred similar scenes on the tube, never imagining they could ever be real.

"Robbie? You are out there?"

Robbie swallowed slowly and went in. John Mack had a small plastic envelope filled with a white powder. He wet his index finger, pushed it into the powder, and lifted it to his lips. He tasted the powder, then he dumped the envelope into a sink and set the water running.

"Does he give a good haircut?" he asked casually.

"What?" Robbie asked, bewildered.

"You were in the barbershop."

"Yes, sir."

"Well, how are the haircuts?"

Robbie managed to smile as he said, "Bogus."

"Oh," John Mack said, looking around thoughtfully. "But then, I'm a little straighter than you, maybe I'd like them. How much does he charge? A good cheap haircut isn't easy to locate these days."

As he spoke, John Mack continued to look around as if he were searching for something.

"Three bucks, plus the tip," Robbie said.

"That's not bad. When I first started paying for my own haircuts the tab was only fifty cents. Of course, that was at the barber college, and they didn't always cut too carefully."

"Was that heroin?" Robbie asked.

"It was. And unless I'm wrong there's some more of it around here somewhere."

John Mack knelt to look under the rim of the sink. He grunted, and then went into the toilet stall and felt behind the tank. "And here it is." He pulled out a larger plastic envelope that had been taped behind the tank. He studied it briefly, then opened it and dumped the contents into the toilet bowl. He flushed it away.

"Are you hungry?" he asked Robbie.

"Yeah . . . I guess so."

"Then let's get out of here."

When they walked through the ping-pong palace, everything was as it had been, just as if nothing had happened.

Out on the street, John Mack asked, "You like dogs?"

"Well, we have a cat—"

"Hotdogs, son. I like them with chili and chopped onions. Puts a breath on you, but I'm not keeping company, if you know what I mean. There's a Nedick's right up here."

"All right," Robbie said. Suddenly he was enjoying himself. John Mack knew his way around the streets, walked there with a special grace that was obvious to Robbie, and was full of subtle and adult secrets he might be willing to share. "I've seen that dude," Robbie said.

"I suppose you have."

"He's always around."

"That's his job. He's a main man."

"A what?"

"A pusher."

"I guessed that."

"Yes, I suppose you did. Well, then, I was just giving him the new ground rules. Telling him to warn his people our building is now off limits. That's why I flushed his stash, so he'd know I was serious. These people live in another world, you know, you can't just talk to them. They think talk's cheap. The only thing that counts with them is a broken head."

They were at the Nedick's, and John Mack ordered a chili dog and an orange soda. Robbie ordered the same. While they were eating, Robbie noticed the butt of a pistol under Mack's coat. Robbie felt a startle of surprise go all through him.

"The only trouble with these things is they're messy to eat," John Mack said, picking up his chili dog. "So how's school?"

"Okay," Robbie said. He didn't want to talk about school.

"You're in the band, aren't you?"

Robbie looked surprised, and John Mack smiled. "I've heard you practicing."

"Yeah, I'm first clarinet."

"You must be pretty good."

"I'm supposed to be. The other kids don't play all that well."

He tried to eat his chili dog the way Mack was eating his, but some of the chili ran out of the wax paper and dripped on the sleeve of his jacket. "Here," Mack said, and handed him a paper napkin. "I don't want your mother blaming me."

"She won't. Don't worry." Robbie took a deep breath and asked, "Why do you have a gun?"

Mack smiled down at him. "You might say it's one of the tools of my trade."

"Would you let me look at it?"

"A gun's not a toy, Robbie. Let's walk over to Riverside Drive and take a look at the water."

They walked across on one of the numbered streets, where the sidewalk was like a corridor between the red brick buildings and the cars parked solidly along the curb, and a block away from the drive they ran into three big kids. Robbie knew the type—too old for school, too young to get jobs, they were bored and always looking for trouble. They were playing sidewalk chicken, coming three abreast, forcing others to step aside and let them pass.

But Mack never paused. "Robbie, get behind me," he said. He seemed to swell slightly. Robbie felt a thrill of excitement. To him Mack seemed like a moving wall of concrete. At the last moment, the kids lost their nerve and broke apart to let Mack and Robbie through.

Robbie heard one of them say, "I didn't know they stacked shit that high."

And another added, "Nor made it stink so bad."

But Mack was smiling. "That's how you can tell a paper-assed punk, Robbie, when they start saying they won when they didn't."

At that moment a beer bottle broke on the street just behind them. Robbie felt Mack scoop him up and move him aside. Then Mack had his coat open and his hand on the butt of the gun, but the kids were running now, laughing.

"What scum," Mack said. "I'd like to go through here with my old platoon and clean this neighborhood out. One sweep and we could make this a decent place to live. Now look at that. Ain't that something?"

They were at the railing across the drive, and below them the Hudson stretched off in both directions. The river was a misty pearl gray, streaked with reflected sunlight, and in mid-channel two small tugs were passing each other. On the Jersey side the huge condos blended almost imperceptibly with the natural rock of the Palisades, and the George Washington Bridge arched across as if it had been thrown from one side to the other.

"This river's always got something to show you," Mack said. "And look there."

Robbie saw Mrs. Jacobs sitting on one of the green city benches, also looking out over the Hudson. They walked toward her. When she saw them, Robbie thought he caught a flicker of consternation on her face. Then she smiled and said, "Hello, John, and hello, Robbie."

Mack was shaking his head with disapproval. "Ida, Ida, what am I going to do with you?"

"But this is the nicest time of day," Mrs. Jacobs said.

"Now what did I tell you?"

Mrs. Jacobs looked guilty. "I know."

Mack turned to Robbie. "Most crimes are committed in the afternoon. That's a fact." He pointed at Mrs. Jacobs's purse, lying beside her on the bench. "And there's your purse, Ida, just like you'd placed an ad, come and rob me."

"But I don't carry any money," she said.

"These punks aren't mind readers."

"But what am I supposed to do? I just can't lock myself in the apartment day after day."

"Come down in the mornings. It's much safer then."

"There's a glare off the water—it hurts my eyes."

John Mack smiled and shook his head. "You're a stone wall, Ida." He looked at his wristwatch and said to Robbie, "I've got to get back."

Mrs. Jacobs stood up. "I think I'll come with you. It seems to be getting colder."

As they walked back toward the building, Mrs. Jacobs said, "I suppose I could come out earlier."

John Mack smiled again. "That's my girl."

CHAPTER SEVEN

Charlie Hyatt was spending Saturday trying to fix a few things. The toilet-paper holder in the hall bath was broken, and a knob was loose on one of the kitchen cabinets. He found his few tools in the lower kitchen drawer. They were mixed in with a tangle of utility wire, and he pulled them loose, trying to remember why he had left the wire unwound. He never took any care of these tools. His own father had been scrupulous. When he used his chisels, he'd sharpened them before he put them away, and he had saved odd nuts and screws in old jelly jars. But he hadn't passed on these habits to Charlie, and when

Robbie grew up he probably wouldn't know a screw-driver from a hand ax.

This thought saddened Charlie. Something was being lost, a tradition and an appreciation for the value of the effort stored up in created things, and he determined to work carefully and solidly. He bought a new holder and screwed it in place. The cabinet knob was stripped, and Charlie remembered how his father had shimmed loose screw holes with a kitchen match, a trick he called a "dutchman." Charlie did the same, using white glue. The knob screwed on solidly, and this pleased him so much he determined to wire the dimmer switch into the Tiffany lamp. He had bought the switch months ago, and Lynn had been after him to install it, but he hadn't found the time. Lynn had wanted the super to do it, and Charlie had said he liked to fix things around his own home, and anyway the job was a snap.

But it wasn't. As soon as he had the faceplate off the regular switch, he saw there were more pairs than there should be, and some of the wires were omi-nously thick. He knew there was 220 wiring in the apartment, because of the air conditioner, and 220 scared him. Why was he being a fool about this? He had many skills, and he made a decent living from them.

He caught Rudy Simbro on his phone in the base-ment, and Rudy said he could come right up. A minute later there was a knock on the door, and Charlie let Rudy in. He carried his toolcase. "Where's your problem, Mr. Hyatt?" Charlie showed him, and Rudy looked at the wires. "Oh, yeah," he said. "I don't think these are live. Anyway, these are the two you want. Yeah, I can get this."

Rudy was a thin, dry man in his late forties, who

always wore khakis that looked a few sizes too large. He often smelled of industrial cleaners, and he usually needed a shave. But he seldom drank, and while he wasn't always cheerful, he was never sour. To talk to him at any time for over five minutes was to learn how he had supered here for over fifteen years and there wasn't a cockroach in the building he didn't know by its first name.

"You want a beer, Rudy?" Charlie asked.

"Nah, I got to go up to Five B. Stopped-up sink. I guess that's an improvement—usually it's their toilet."

Lynn came in from shopping with her arms full of different-size bags. She put the bags on the table, saw what Rudy was doing, looked at Charlie, and decided not to say anything.

"Hi, honey. Hello, Rudy."

"How are you, Mrs. Hyatt?"

"Fine."

"Has it been warm enough for you in here?"

"Yes, except for a couple of those cold nights."

"They need a new furnace This one's been here since before I came, and it's limping. I tell them, but nothing happens."

"We were okay, Rudy," Charlie said. Then he turned to Lynn. "What did you buy?"

She smiled wickedly. "Everything."

"Oh, no."

"Everything was a bargain. I even found a sale on vitamin E."

"Great."

"Where's Robbie?" Lynn asked.

"I don't know. Probably over at Jonathon's."

Rudy interrupted, "He's downstairs."

There was something in Rudy's tone that caused Charlie to ask, "What do you mean?"

85

"He's in the basement with John Mack. I saw him there on my way up."

Charlie thought for a moment, then said, "I think I'll take a look"

Lynn asked, "Why? What's the matter?"

"I don't know."

Charlie went swiftly downstairs, thinking with some pleasure how light he still was on the steps. Jesus, how long had it been since they'd gone dancing? He came out in the basement corridor, with its flat-green walls and oil-stained concrete. He knew Mack had fixed up an office down here, and it was probably in the old storage room. He heard Mack's voice before he opened the door. ". . . Now this is your safety bar. It blocks the hammer at all times."

Charlie pushed the door open and saw Mack and Robbie sitting on a small cot. A desk sat on the other side of the room, and on a TV monitor he could see the empty lobby. Mack had a Police Special broken open, showing it to Robbie, and Robbie was asking, "Is that important?"

"Absolutely," Mack said, "you want to make sure that when you shoot it's on purpose. No accidents that way." Mack looked up. "Hello, Mr. Hyatt."

Robbie turned around, his eyes showing surprise. "Hi, Dad."

"Why don't you go upstairs and see if you can help your mother," Charlie said.

"Now?" The boy was obviously disappointed.

"Right now."

"Okay . . ." Robbie turned back to John Mack. "Thanks a lot, John."

"That's okay, Robbie," Mack said, without taking his eyes off Charlie.

"You go on, Robbie, I'll be along in a minute."

Charlie waited until he heard Robbie on the stairs, before he looked at Mack. Then he said, "The next time you show Robbie a gun, ask me first."

Mack's eyes were placid. "There was no danger, sir. I removed the cartridges."

"That's not the point. We don't like guns in our family."

"Well, to each his own. Some parents have their kids on the range by the time they're Robbie's age."

"Not these parents."

"Like you say, sir."

There was something about Mack that annoyed Charlie, but he forced himself to overcome it. "Look, I don't want to make a federal case out of this. I'm sure he was bugging you."

Mack crossed to his desk and opened the drawer, where he had a box of shells. He began to reload the gun. "Most kids have a natural curiosity about firearms. Next time he brings it up, I'll just change the subject."

"Thanks."

In the open drawer Charlie saw a strange knife next to the box of ammo. It was crude and raw-looking, and the handle was wrapped with electrician's tape

"What's that?" Charlie asked.

"A shank." Mack picked the knife up and handed it to Charlie. "It's a street weapon, the kind they make in jail."

Charlie saw that the thing had been made from a file, crudely ground to an edge. Involuntarily he imagined what it would be like to catch this in the gut. "Ugly," he said. "Where'd you get it?"

"I found it in the alley, near the back door of the building."

For a moment he sensed the hungry life all around him out there on the streets. People who wanted what he had. "It's never far away, is it?" he said.

Mack finished loading his gun and replaced it in his holster. He took the knife from Charlie and said, "There's a lot of these out there. Every punk on the street carrys something sharp."

Charlie thought he caught the indelible tones of a commercial. On the monitor he saw Morrison coming in with his dog Mack leaned over to watch carefully.

Charlie laughed and said, "I'll have to tell Morrison I saw him on the tube."

"What?" Mack asked.

"Nothing. I'll see you around, John."

"Okay, sir. Any problems, you call me, right?"

At dinner that night, he asked Robbie what he'd been doing with John Mack.

"Just hanging out with him," Robbie said.

"I could see that. But what did you do?"

"Charlie," Lynn interrupted, "you sound like he's on trial."

"Well, that man seems a little unusual to me. I guess I'm just trying to get a better feel of him. I'm sorry, Robbie, I didn't mean to force my way into your space."

Robbie looked grave. He knew all this talk of individual rights was very important to his parents. "That's okay, Dad, we didn't do much He bought me a chili dog, and we walked over to take a look at the river. One thing, though, he faced down three dudes who wanted to crowd us off the sidewalk, and he made it look like nothing."

"Yeah," Charlie said dryly, remembering his own recent encounter.

"I'll tell you the truth," Lynn said, "and I didn't think I'd be saying this, but I feel safer with him around. He's *here*, you know what I mean?"

"Well," Charlie said, aware that his tone was grudging, and unable to help it, "he costs enough. Let's hope he continues to be worth it." Then, deliberately changing the subject, he asked Lynn, "Have we got everything we need tonight? Ice? Soda?"

They were giving a small party. For a long time whenever they gave a party they had asked everyone they knew, just to prove they were popular, and every party had been the same drunken scramble. Now they gave smaller parties, a few people, carefuly chosen. They both agreed that a party was a living design, kinetic art, with a subtle theme. Tonight was bringing in the Julians and the Chamberses to meet a few of the people from Charlie's show.

Lynn smiled and studied Charlie's question for a moment. "I'm just afraid we won't have enough to eat."

Charlie laughed heartily, and Robbie said, "Mom, you always *worry* and there's always stuff left over."

"If your mother had barrels of dip and bushels of chips, she'd still *worry* someone would show up with a pet elephant and clean her out. *Worry about* booze, that's the thing to worry about "

"Oh, I know you *worry about* that, so I don't have to."

The party was going well—the Julians and the Chamberses seemed to be having a good time—and Charlie was feeling no pain. He'd busied himself bringing drinks and taking care of the music, stopping to talk to everyone as he passed. He was changing a record when Lynn came up with her party smile to whisper, "Baby, don't play *Sergeant Pepper*. Everyone's not as crazy about that as you are."

"It's a classic."

"I know, but you play it and play it. Please put on something neutral."

"How about Ned Negative and the Nihilists?"

"Be nice."

"Maybe the Sex Pistols, they got a great new one called *Everybody Died*."

"Charlie, please."

"Okay, some cautious neutrality coming up."

He looked along the backs of the records until he came to Richard Dyer-Bennett in a collection of Elizabethan folk songs. Amused at this choice, he removed the record from the sleeve.

"Hey, Charlie, have you seen Asher's new play?"

He turned to find George Placer bent over him. George topped six six, and his small, neat head and slender, almost tubular body made him look like a praying mantis

"No, how is it?"

"Gloriously chaotic. In the last act they destroy the scenery."

Charlie smiled as he set the needle. "They must not be planning to run very long."

"Well, of course the *Times* japed them, but they expected that. The *Voice* was kind, but you know how patronizing they are."

"Reviewers always have to make sure you understand they're superior to the material, whatever it is."

"What's that?" George asked.

"It's an occupational disability—"

"No, I mean the music."

"Oh, nothing, George. You know, I always suspected Jerry Asher might be a small talent inside a large ego."

George Placer straightened up, suddenly even taller, and looked down along his narrow nose. "That may be, Charlie, but then, time is exposing more than a few of us, isn't it, and at least Asher's writing plays."

Charlie took a sip of his drink and said quietly, "Now you're beating me with my own shield."

Placer laughed, and his small eyes flickered with appreciation. "I know what you mean, Charlie "

Charlie noticed Lynn opening the front door, and he wondered who could be arriving this late. He was surprised to see John Mack come in. And he looked grim. He was hatless, and his shirt was pulled half out of his pants. He went directly to the Julians, spoke to them briefly. Charlie saw Claire's eyes widen and her mouth open in dismay. Then the three were leaving.

"Excuse me, George, something's going on," Charlie said, and went over to where Lynn was still looking out the door. "What is it?" he asked.

"Someone broke into the Julians' apartment."

"No shit?"

Charlie ran down to see if he could help. He found the door open, and stepped inside. "Jesus," he said softly. The apartment had been trashed. The stereo had been smashed, the TV kicked in, and the paintings wrenched from the walls and ripped against the sharp points of the modern furniture. Smashed glass was everywhere. The houseplants had been thrown against the white brick of the fireplace, the pots shattered, the plants uprooted, dirt everywhere. The model summer home, still sitting in the middle of the glass coffee table, had been jumped on, demolished in a savage dance.

When she saw this, Claire Julian, always so careful to appear poised, burst into tears. "Now why did they have to break that?" she said.

Julian looked stunned, but he had had far more experience with the violent and the unexpected than his wife. "This is a horror show," he said. He turned to John Mack, who was standing to the side, a little like a tour guide. "How'd they get in here?" Julian asked.

"Through the kitchen window, sir."

Without his hat, Mack looked more ordinary, a strong man on the edge of middle age. His hair was cut as he had probably worn it in the service, short on the sides, a little longer on top, and still neatly parted, but he was fifteen pounds over his best weight. His eyes were steady and respectful and his voice carefully neutral.

They went into the kitchen to look at the entry. Charlie saw that the bars had been ripped out of the smashed concrete. "How the hell did they do that?" Charlie asked.

"Probably a jack," Mack said.

"What do you mean?" asked Julian.

"A lot of them use a car jack. Not a bumper jack, but one of the old-fashioned ones that went under the axle." Mack walked to the window and demonstrated with an imaginary jack. "You see, they put the jack between the bars and just crank them open."

Chambers came into the kitchen. "So that's how he got in."

"There were two of them, sir."

Charlie stepped forward and leaned across the sink to check the size of the window with his hands. "This is a really tight squeeze."

92

John Mack said, "Most junkies are so thin they have to stand twice to throw a shadow."

No one smiled at this. Julian said, "Tell me exactly what happened, John."

Mack assumed the tone he must have used when he once reported to a superior officer. "I was making my usual rounds when I heard some banging inside your apartment. I knew you were up at the Hyatts', so I went outside to see if I could see anything through the windows. The blinds were closed in front, but in the alley I found broken glass, and the bars were wrenched out. So I came through—"

"You came through that window?" Charlie asked.

"There's little tricks to that sort of thing, sir. Anyway, they must have heard me coming, because they dropped everything and ran out the front door. I probably made a mistake, coming through the window —it took me too long. They were on their way out, and moving fast."

"Did you get a decent look at them?" Chambers asked.

"I couldn't pick them out of a lineup. I chased them through the lobby and out onto the sidewalk. I might have caught one of them, but I figured my first responsibility was to the building here. You know, those kids are like Poland hogs, they all look the same. They had long hair and jeans, and that's about what I saw. You got a phone in here?"

"Right there, John."

"Doctor, you'd better make an inventory. The police will need to know if anything is missing. I don't think they got anything. They dropped some of that stuff as they were busting out of here, and everything seems okay in the bedroom, but you'd better check and make sure."

"All right, John," Julian said. "And, look, John, thanks for not rubbing this in."

"What, sir?"

"You warned me about security, and I didn't listen to you."

Mack's expression didn't change as he said, "The important thing is that no one was hurt."

"Yes, we're grateful."

"Thank you, sir."

Mack began to call the police, and the rest of them automatically started back to the living room. Charlie couldn't get over how ugly it was. He remembered how the apartment had been the night they had had drinks with the Julians and looked over the model of the house they were building in the Hamptons. That night the apartment had been almost frigid in its perfection. Now it was chaos. Reduced to trash by an act of nature as random and capricious as an earthquake.

In the living room, Lynn was comforting Claire and several members of the party were standing in the open door, staring around in dismayed surprise. Charlie moved close to Julian and said quietly, "Is there some way I can help?"

"Oh, no, thanks, Charlie. I'll have it cleaned up and replaced. What the hell. It's just more stuff to buy, isn't it? I have home owners insurance, so it's covered, even if I lose a little to inflation. So we're not hurt physically."

Charlie glanced at Claire, who was trying to pull herself together. She couldn't be comfortable crying in front of strangers, and she was drying her eyes carefully with a blue Kleenex. "I'm going to get these people out of here," Charlie said privately to Julian. "Take care."

He moved his guests back upstairs, to find the

party breaking up. George Placer stayed on for a last drink, and Charlie sat and talked quietly about some of the things they had done in the Village ten years ago. His voice took on a special fondness when he told early Village stories, but he knew the glow of these *events* was reflected from the energy of his own youth, when he was still possibly anyone he might imagine himself to be, before *events* had begun to define him. Placer was an agreeable listener, well acquainted with Charlie's cast of characters, and he sat swirling the ice in his drink, smiling with real pleasure over Charlie's turns of phrase. One thing recalled another. How rich their lives seemed, if he didn't make the effort to remember that these events had occurred many months apart.

Lynn came back, and George Placer got up to leave. "Don't go on my account," Lynn said.

"I'll walk you to your cab," Charlie said. "I want to get a paper, anyway."

When they stepped out of the building, the night air was still warm, and the streets looked like reddish caverns. There was a fresh smell of spring, probably drifting across from the New Jersey countryside. Charlie took a deep breath and thought that he spent too much time inside. He really needed a week away. A time to think. George was out in the street, looking for a cab, and he went over to him and said, "That was a petty remark I made about Asher."

George nodded with sympathetic understanding. "I admire Asher because he gets the energy together and takes the chance—" He broke off; an empty cab was cruising along half a block away. "I'll see you, Charlie."

"Yes, take care."

Charlie walked across the street and down toward

the newsstand on the corner. Behind the wooden counter he saw Fletch, the vendor, and Rudy Simbro bent over a game of chess. Fletch was one of those wizards who play without looking at the board, but nature had provided his blindfold. His sightless eyes were sheltered behind large, round, very dark glasses. When Charlie paused in front of the counter, Fletch looked up, smiled, and said, "Good evening, Mr. Hyatt."

"That's amazing," Charlie said.

Fletch nodded his head with the satisfaction of an acknowledged sage. "I got your walk down."

Rudy Simbro was studying his move, but he laid out a fast, dry aside. "He's shitting you, Mr. Hyatt. I told him you were coming."

The line of Fletch's mouth turned faintly sour. "Just move, duck, I got you by the short hairs, and don't you just know it." His hand reached up for Charlie's money and made change for a one, just as if he could see it. But of course, Charlie realized, anyone who handed a five or a ten to a blind news vendor would be pretty sure to say what it was. "You had cops over there again, did you?" Fletch asked idly.

"Yeah," Charlie said, "third time this month. They're thinking about making it a substation. Well, you must have seen some of it?"

Fletch laughed out loud. "Not me."

"No, I mean Rudy, of course. Rudy, you didn't see anything?"

Rudy was trying to decide whether he wanted to move a knight or a bishop. "Any what? What do you mean?"

"How long have you been here?" Charlie asked.

"Couple of hours. This is our third game."

"One apiece," Fletch said. "This is the rubber."

Charlie ignored that. "This would have been around ten, maybe ten-thirty?"

Rudy caught the change in Charlie's tone, and it reminded him that he was the super and Charlie was an important tenant. "I haven't noticed anything."

"Two dudes came running out the front door, and they must have been going like they had a bear after them. You didn't see them?"

Rudy shook his head firmly. "No, sir, not by me. I was right here. I saw the people who came for the party and I saw the cops when they showed, but there was nothing more except for the usual traffic. What happened?"

"They ripped off the Julians' apartment and smashed it into junk. A pretty ugly job."

"Jesus, I don't know, Mr. Hyatt, I can't be one hundred percent certain, but I'm almost sure nobody like that came out of our building, and if they had and I saw them, I'd at least call John Mack. I mean, that's his territory now, ain't it?"

Charlie thought a moment, then said, "Sure, Rudy, thanks."

"That switch working okay?"

"Yeah. Very nice. Thanks a lot."

Usually he opened the paper to scan the top of the news, reading history in the angular language of subheads, but tonight he tucked it under his arm. He walked quickly, watching the sidewalk automatically, as he realized that there was something about the burglary that troubled him. He was almost to his door before he saw John Mack standing there. Mack was watching him, had been watching him.

"Nice night," Charlie said.

Mack then turned to stare up at the tops of the

buildings across the street. "It doesn't stay fresh long, does it?"

"No, I guess it doesn't."

"This city's like a stew," Mack said, still looking up across the street. "It simmers all spring, and by summer it begins to boil."

Charlie smiled at the image. Mack looked directly at him and continued in a different tone. "Do you go out for a newspaper every night?"

"Most nights, yes."

"That's dangerous, sir."

"Come on, John, we're not in Nam anymore."

"Aren't we?"

"No, we're not," Charlie said sharply. He couldn't be certain, but Mack seemed to have hardened slightly toward him since their talk in the basement, when he had told him not to show Robbie a gun. There was a slight edge to his style, very like the tone a rule-book sergeant might use with an officer he didn't respect. Well, let him boil his head, Charlie thought.

"I'm going in," he said, and went upstairs. He was surprised to find Lynn in the living room with a drink in her hand. Her drink made it much easier to pour his own. "Charlie, that was just grotesque," Lynn said.

Charlie took a deep swallow, and the still-undiluted Scotch was warm and comforting in his throat. "That's the word," he said absently.

"I feel like we were living in a disaster area. It's like being bombed. How long can they go on missing you?"

He sensed the heat of her distress and put his drink down immediately to go put his arms around her. She tossed her shoulders. "Oh, that won't help," she said.

He held her anyway, amazed as he sometimes was at the tension in her small body, and after a moment she relaxed in his arms. He realized that in some elemental core she depended upon him for *protection* even when she knew their lives were constantly threatened by events from which there was no possible *protection*. Tragedy whispered everywhere. The news was little more than an ongoing scenario of different cataclysms, great and small, and no matter how diminished things seemed on the screen, as if they were not watching real disasters but only clever miniatures, in the unconscious, which recorded everything, they lived their lives in a constant state of siege. Any day their world could blow up just as completely as if the entire planet had been destroyed.

They began to make love on the couch. They hadn't fucked out here in several years, and Charlie found it exciting. The couch was firmer than their bed, and that made his stroke seem harder. The bull in his glory. He could tell from her breathing that it was going to work, and he closed his eyes, gathered her up, and just went into it. There was another world in there he couldn't always reach.

CHAPTER EIGHT

Sue Kramer wasn't impressed with John Mack. He was all over the building, getting into everything, and she didn't like the feel of him. Sue was a passionate libber, and she recognized in Mack the outlines of the essential enemy. Not only did he smell of MCP, she also had the instinct that he was smuggling some darker and stranger stench, hidden deep in his underwear. She was used to being stared at, expected this, but there was something distinctly unpleasant in the way Mack looked at her. As if she were contaminated meat.

She had her first open confrontation with Mack. Stu

had been over most of the afternoon. Stu was good-looking and passive, but there was a pretty sharp clock ticking away behind his mild blue eyes, and she had asked him to read her thesis. "Dig into it," she had said, "and tell me what you really think. I have to know if all the legs are solid."

Stu had sat in her canvas wing chair with his ankles crossed, first one way, then the other, reading steadily. Her study ran over fifty pages, and she wasn't going to sit staring at him, trying to read his expression, so she said, "I have to do some wash. If you need anything, you know where it is."

He looked up and smiled briefly. "Okay."

She gathered her dirty clothes and went down to the basement. To reach the laundry room she had to pass the old storage room where Mack had made his office. The door was open, and he was sitting there at the desk, reading a magazine. He looked up automatically as she passed, and their eyes met briefly. He didn't speak, and neither did she. That was just as well. There was something too humble about his "yes, sirs" and "yes, ma'ams," and Sue preferred the security of open antagonism. Then she dismissed him, and as she put in her wash, she began to recapitulate the arguments and illustrations Stu was now following.

She had attempted to trace the inevitable economic implications of political oppression of all varieties, to show how at base they were identical. Always one group was trying to steal the labor of another. Cut through the rhetoric, the dogma, and all social systems could be seen as instruments of exploitation. She felt she had grasped a hard and unpleasant truth, and one she was sure some of her professors would meet with hostility. She had to be sure she had made the best case possible.

She was sorting her underwear, holding up a pair of bikini pants to check them for wear, when she became aware of someone in the corridor. Immediately, unbidden, the rape that had happened right here flared into her mind. She had studied martial arts at the women's center and knew tricks Fran had lacked, but she also knew there were many men too powerful to fight. This was a simple fact of nature.

She turned, trying to control her own instinctive alarm, to find John Mack looking in at her. She still held the bikinis, holding them now as if she were offering them to him, and she saw the flicker in his face. For a moment she saw the bikinis as he might see them, too flimsy to be anything more than a bit of sexual decoration, something for a man to savor before she slipped them off and revealed herself completely.

Mack nodded shortly, and withdrew. The son of a bitch, she thought. He's smarter than he looks. And he's careful.

When she returned to her apartment, Stu had about ten pages left to read. She went into the kitchen and began to make toasted cheese sandwiches. She interrupted him to ask, "Do you want coffee?"

He nodded.

She went on, "All I have is instant."

"That's fine."

She played with the sandwiches, spreading the bread first with cream cheese, which she dusted with hot Hungarian paprika. She filled the center with thin-sliced Muenster, and buttered the outsides. She enjoyed designing food more than she enjoyed eating it, and she went on to slice up a small tomato, which she added to the cheese. She fried the sandwiches carefully in her large iron skillet, catching them just as they were turning golden brown. She smiled over this small satisfaction.

As they ate, Stu told her the thesis was "brilliant." She studied him doubtfully, wondering why it was so difficult to accept just what she had hoped to hear. She accused him of timidity. Then she accused him of gutlessness. Finally she said, "You're afraid to be critical for fear I won't make a pass at you."

He smiled slowly as he said, "Criticism would guarantee that, I think."

"Oh," she said, "that's naughty."

Something changed in his face. The change was slight, but at the same time profound.

"Did you mean to be naughty?" she asked.

He put his half-eaten sandwich on the edge of his plate and sat silently, eyes down.

"I think you did," she said, with the kindly severity of a mother correcting a three-year-old. "Well, I guess we don't want our nice lunch that Mommy worked so hard to fix, I guess we want something else . . ."

She saw that he was beginning to shiver, and she felt a flicker of excitement, like a flow of heat, running over her skin.

"Do we want to take our pants down because we've been naughty?"

He whimpered, and she got up to walk around and stand over him, menacing him with her presence. She went on, whispering now, getting into the grossness of the characterization she was creating. "Do we want to take our pants off and show Mommy our pretty pink balls—"

"Oh, *Sue!*" he snapped, with sudden violence. "Don't get cute!"

She glared at him, and he went on in an easier tone. "Don't you understand, it doesn't work unless you take it seriously."

"I can't, you know, it's just a game, and games are supposed to be fun."

"Fear is a lot of fun. I'm serious."

Despite this, they managed to get to bed. He lay on his back, and she rode him for a long time, like a teenage girl riding a large, gentle white horse, controlling all that warm and powerful flesh. It went on like that to the end, and when the ride was over, she lay beside him wishing he would leave. He was sensitive, and in a moment he was up getting dressed. She put on a robe and saw him to the door. The wetness between her legs was now disagreeable.

He kissed her briefly and said, "Your paper's hot stuff."

The remark surprised her. "Thank you. It makes me happy to hear you say that, and you know, I don't mean to be so symptomatic."

"Neither do I. Maybe we should talk about that sometime. Take care."

She was closing the door to set the lock when she heard another voice.

"Just a minute."

She knew who that was, and reopened the door. Mack was at the head of the stairs, effectively blocking Stu's way.

"My name is John Mack," he was saying. "I'm responsible for security here."

"Yes?" Stu said, and she could hear the effort it cost him to keep his voice firm.

"I notice you've been dropping by to see Miss Kramer. Isn't this the second time this week?"

Sue stepped out in the hall, holding her robe closed with one hand. "Are you keeping a record or are you keeping score?" she asked.

Both men turned to look at her. Stu made an expression as if to say "Now what's this?" and Mack looked her over with those flat cop eyes, noting the robe, noting the flesh above her jugs. She prevented herself from adjusting the robe and pulling it more securely over her nakedness. She stared back at him.

"This young man seems to have a key to the front door."

Sue said, "That's right. I gave it to him."

"We have a rule, miss."

"Fuck your rule," she said flatly.

"It's not *my* rule, it's the house rule."

"No one voted on that."

"Miss, we had a burglary the other night, thousands of dollars' worth of damage, and I'm here to prevent that sort of thing."

"You didn't prevent that one, did you?"

Stu was getting uncomfortable. Mack was still blocking his way. "Look, what do you want from me?"

"I'd like that key, son."

"Don't give it to him!"

Stu's eyes were bleak. "This isn't my hassle." He took out his ring and began to remove her key. She couldn't prevent herself from saying, "Why don't you give him your balls, too?"

She rushed into her apartment, slammed the door, and leaned with her back against it for ten seconds, and then she went back out on the landing and ran to the head of the stairs. Mack was halfway down the flight. She yelled at his back, "What I do with my keys and my life is my business. I'm not in the army."

Mack didn't even look back. He turned down below and walked out of sight. In a moment she heard his heavy step on the next flight.

CHAPTER NINE

Rudy Simbro also heard footsteps that night. He was out late. Nights were a problem for him. He didn't sleep much, and there was no one to talk to except Fletch, and sometimes he was tired of huddling in that coop. On those nights he sat in the White Rose, drinking small beers and watching sports on the over-sized screen along with a whole barful of worn and unsuccessful middle-aged men just like himself, men who had never had wives or children, or if they had, they'd left them years ago in some other city.

Rudy seldom got any conversation going here. Once in a while someone would say something to

him, turn to him and ask him how he'd liked some
flashy play, but the talk never went anywhere. They
didn't talk much. They sat and watched and discussed
what they saw in a limited and laconic code.

—Hey, did you see that?

—Yeah, wasn't that something.

—Sure was.

But while Rudy sat there he was part of it. He
drank a few beers and, as a treat, took a shot with his
last. Then he counted his change, left a quarter, and
walked over to use the cigarette machine on his way
out. He dropped his coins carefully, listening for the
click of each one. The little mechanism that caused
the machine to discriminate between nickles, dimes,
and quarters was out of adjustment, and unless you
gave it a lot of time it went crazy and gave up. Rudy
was sensitive to its problem, and he was rewarded
when the lever pulled and the red pack dropped out.

He picked up the cigarettes and felt for matches.

He straightened and called to the bartender, "Hey,
this thing used to give you matches."

The bartender shrugged as he said, "They *used* to
give you free boiled eggs and pickles."

The streets seemed quiet after the noise of the television. Only a few cars hummed by on the avenue,
most of them off-duty cabs running for the barn. The
air was damp with the mist off the river, and there
was a touch of chill in it. Rudy walked along, smoking and feeling mellow after the shot he'd put down.
The shop windows were dark, most of them barricaded against burglars, and the trash cans lined the
sidewalks like misshapen monuments. Two kids he
immediately tagged as students, therefore safe, came
out of an all-night pizzeria. The boy was clowning
and the girl was laughing at him. Her laughter fol-

lowed Rudy as he walked along, growing gradually fainter. He turned the corner and was alone on the street. The building was three blocks away.

In the middle of the first block he heard footsteps behind him. This time of night he checked everything, so he looked around. But he didn't see anyone. Twice more he thought he heard something, and looked around to find the street empty behind him. You're getting jumpy, he told himself. But he picked up his pace, walking along briskly. The building was just ahead, just beyond the alley. The mouth of the alley was dark, and he automatically began to skirt out around it. Then he heard someone moving very swiftly, and when he turned this last time, he was shoved sharply from behind. He fell forward, face down. Someone grabbed him by the collar and pulled him rapidly into the dark shadows of the alley. It was like being seized by a large animal.

Rudy was aware of a bulky shadow over him, and then a light exploded in his head. Then another. He heard the bones breaking in his cheeks.

CHAPTER TEN

Charlie Hyatt was at the studio when he heard Rudy Simbro had been *beaten*. Lynn called, and he took it in the booth. She said immediately, "Rudy Simbro was mugged last night, and *beaten* so badly he's still in the hospital."

"Jesus. Where'd it happen?"

"In the alley next to the building. From what I heard, he wasn't found until this morning. He was still unconscious when the trash men came by. They called the police."

"What is going on?"

"I don't know," Lynn said. "But I'm getting scared.

I thought you'd want to know about this, and I was wondering if I should do anything. Like send flowers or go in to see him."

Charlie shook his head, forgetting Lynn couldn't note the gesture. "I'll try to go by, and Rudy's not the flower type. He'll want smokes and maybe some magazines. Where's he at?"

"Columbia General."

"All right, I'll drop in on the way home. See you tonight. And, look, try not to worry."

"I do try, Charlie."

Charlie hung up and looked thoughtfully at the control panel without seeing it. Someone came up to ask him how he wanted to block the next series of shots, and he turned his mind to work.

Columbia General was only two blocks from his subway stop, and he decided he should look in on Rudy. Poor bastard. When the muggers started going for game as lean as Rudy, times were hard. Charlie stopped at the kiosk on the subway platform and bought several sports magazines and a copy of *People*. In the corridor outside Rudy's ward, he ran into Lieutenant Yeager. Yeager wore the same clothes and the same harried expression.

"Lieutenant," Charlie said. "I don't suppose you remember me?"

Yeager shot him a quick look. "I'm afraid not."

"Charles Hyatt. There was a shooting in my building a month ago. You and your people came by."

"Oh, sure, the Wallace thing." Yeager jerked his head at the door of the ward. "That fellow in there's your super, isn't he?"

"Yeah. How is he?"

"He took a savage beating."

"Any leads?"

"Nah, it was dark. He didn't see much."

"I don't suppose you caught those kids who killed Wallace, either."

"No, we didn't. By the way, if you're going in there, you should know his jaw's broken. They got his mouth wired shut, so he can't do too much talking."

Yeager put his notebook in his inside coat pocket and turned to go. Charlie said, "Just a minute. Are you sure it was a mugging?"

"Mr. Hyatt, there's a lot of anger in this city. It's exploding all the time. Simbro's watch and his money are gone, so I write that down as a mugging. Why do you ask?"

"I'm not sure."

Charlie found Rudy in an eight-bed ward. It was a moment before he recognized him under the bandages. He walked along the beds looking into the faces of the men lying there. Some obviously were very sick. Charlie suddenly realized how awful it was to be poor and old and sick. There was less care for those who needed the most. Charlie's Guild health plan guaranteed he would always be safe in the semi-private rooms. One fat old man was creeping toward his bed in a walker, his eyes bleak with misery.

Rudy looked awful, as if he had been systematically beaten. Both eyes were puffed nearly shut, and his jaw was wired. Even his forehead was bruised.

"Rudy . . ." Charlie said.

He saw that Rudy was looking at him, and he went on quickly, "Don't try to talk. I just came by to bring you something to pass the time, and to see how you were."

Rudy managed to whisper, "Pretty low, Mr. Hyatt."

"Do you need anything?"

"No, my sister's been here."

Charlie sat looking at Rudy. What could he say? Down the ward, the old man had reached his bed and was now struggling to get into it, gasping and sighing with the effort.

"Rudy, who did this?"

He thought he saw something flicker in the slits of Rudy's eyes, but Rudy said only, "Dark. Took me from behind."

"Did you fight? I mean, why did they beat you?"

Rudy moved his head slightly, from side to side. After a moment he continued with some difficulty. "Don't know."

Charlie nodded and smiled. He knew he couldn't torment Rudy over some vague feelings of his own. He put the magazines on the bedside stand as he said, "You need to rest, Rudy. I'll try to get back to-morrow."

"Thanks, Mr. Hyatt."

"That's okay. Rest and get well."

He left quickly, careful not to look at the other patients. He walked the few blocks over to the building, glad for the moment to be able to walk. He stopped once, to buy a bottle of wine for dinner. The liquor store had a nice buy on an estate-bottled Bordeaux. The thought of the wine cheered him, and he was smiling as he stepped through the front door and ran into John Mack on his way out. Charlie was developing the habit of avoiding Mack, but now he stopped and said, "Hello, John. Did you hear what happened to Rudy?"

"Yes, I did. It's a jungle just outside that door, Mr. Hyatt."

"Yes, it's beginning to seem like that." He looked carefully at Mack's large white hands. They were unswollen and unmarked. "Well," he went on, "dinner's waiting."

"Yes, sir, I hope you enjoy it."

Upstairs, he found Robbie watching the box and Lynn sitting in the corner of the couch, smoking a cigarette. "Not you?" he said.

She took another puff. "Why not me?"

"Did you buy a pack?"

"Yes, but I took one and threw the rest away."

"Well, where'd you throw them? I'll have one too."

"They're in the kitchen trash."

He fished the pack out of the tangle of wadded wrapping paper, made a drink, and stood in the middle of the kitchen, smoking. He hid himself because he knew it disappointed Robbie when he broke down and smoked. The cigarette made him dizzy for a moment, and he stood quietly, half enjoying the rush. Sometimes life seemed a complex joke. He was sure he smoked because Bogart had smoked. He had watched Bogart manipulate that cigarette as if it were the potent symbol of his essential male worth, and he had never once considered what a foolish and essentially frivolous habit it was, nor did he often remember how Bogart, the real man, had died.

When he returned to the living room, carrying his drink, Lynn asked, "Did you see Rudy?"

"Yes, he's badly beaten, and that hospital's a real animal farm. The worst part of sick is being in there."

"How long does Rudy have to stay?"

"A week, anyway, probably longer."

"Hey, Dad," Robbie joined in, "you know what John says about that whole thing?"

"No, you mean Mr. Mack?"

"He said I could call him John, and he said Rudy

117

Simbro was a zip damn fool to be out on the streets that late at night, without some backup."

"Is that what he said? What else did he have to say?"

"Oh, nothing much. He says according to the cops the muggings have gone up about twenty-five percent. He says it's the inflation."

"Well, he's a mine of bad news, isn't he. When'd you see him? I thought you had practice today."

Robbie had turned back to the TV. "I did. I saw him after."

"Where?"

"I go down and see him."

Charlie suppressed the impulse to tell Robbie not to hang around Mack, but he didn't like his doing it. He was surprised at how much he didn't like it.

Robbie turned and looked up again. "The concert's going to be next Friday," he said.

"That's good. We'll make it."

"I'm playing some dixieland on *Hello, Dolly*."

"That's wonderful. How's it going?"

"Pretty good."

Robbie went back to his program again, and Charlie turned to Lynn to say, "I've always liked dixieland. It's such good-natured music."

"Yes, I suppose it is," she said.

"What's a matter?" he asked.

"I just feel oppressed. I'm going to put dinner together."

"Can I help?"

"No, you relax. There's not much left to do."

He thought about what Lynn had said. *Oppression* was just the right word. It was as though there was a large angry force somewhere around them. He kept catching intimations of it. Periodically it errupted in fits of violence. That was the theme that tied across the Julian burglary and Rudy's mugging. Both betrayed an irrational violence. Charlie could understand why someone might break into Julian's apartment, like breaking into a fancy and exclusive store, but nothing actually had been stolen. The expensive goods had only been destroyed. Why was it necessary to beat Rudy senseless to seize a few bucks and a cheap watch? It didn't make sense to Charlie, and finally, that was what was making him uneasy.

CHAPTER ELEVEN

Violence struck again six days later. Charlie was able to reconstruct the incident from half a dozen different versions. He made it a point to talk to everyone who knew anything about it. The details appeared to be fairly simple and all on the surface. It was early afternoon, and a new couple was moving into the Murphys' old apartment. They had arrived with a big van and moving men, who had found it convenient to prop the door open while they worked. A sneak thief had seized this opportunity to get inside.

Fran was with John Mack when he discovered the open door. She had asked Mack to walk her to and from the laundry room. She had told him she knew it was foolish of her, and he had been very understanding. "You just have to give that some time, Mrs. Jeffries."

"Well, I'd like to give you something. Do you smoke cigars?"

"Not really."

"How about a bottle of wine?"

"No, that's all right, Mrs. Jeffries, this is my job, but I do appreciate the kindness of your thought."

It was at that point he saw the open door and said, "Excuse me."

She had stood watching him, admiring his instant alertness. He went to the door and began to speak to a dark-haired middle-aged man who was standing there with a cardboard carton full of books. "Mr. Andriola?"

"Yes."

"John Mack. I didn't expect you until tomorrow."

"It worked out better for today. I'm sorry—"

"How long has this door been open like this?" Mack asked.

"I don't know. A while."

"Did anyone come in?"

"No, I don't think so," Mr. Andriola said, but his wife, who looked just like him, came up in time to hear the last question, and she said, "Yes, someone did, just a few minutes ago."

"Describe them?" Mack said briskly.

"Oh—"

"Man or a woman."

"A man," Mrs. Andriola said gratefully. "Yes, a man, a young man. He looked like he might be Spanish, or maybe part Spanish."

Mack frowned. "Did you notice whether he went upstairs or downstairs."

"Oh, upstairs. I passed him on the first flight. That's how I noticed him."

Mack immediately started upstairs, pausing to check the halls and landings. Fran followed him until she reached her own apartment, and then she locked herself in, and poured herself a drink. She knew nothing more until she heard the sound of shots above her.

When Charlie came in from work that night, Lynn was out at the superette getting some chili powder, and it was Robbie who told him the news. He came in to find Robbie, still wearing his jacket, looking out the front windows. Robbie turned away as soon as he saw Charlie and came across the room, smiling. "Hey, dad, there was a shooting here, just a little while ago. The cops were here and everything, and, dad, they've taken John down to the station."

Charlie's first thought was *Not again*. He felt an icy flicker of dismay. Then he saw that Robbie was still smiling. He was immediately angry with the boy.

"Wipe that silly grin off your face and tell me what happened."

"I don't know that much, dad. The ambulance was here when I came home. People said another rapist had got into the building and that John, Mr. Mack, had to shoot him."

"Did you see this guy?"

"Yes, when they brought him down."

"What'd he look like?"

Robbie moved his shoulders. "I never saw anyone who was dead before. He didn't look too different. There was a lot of blood and yuck."

"What kind of a person did he look like?"

"Oh, street trash, dad."

Charlie saw that to Robbie the dead man was only a detail in an adventure. This wasn't the time to try to get him to see it any differently. The best thing was to stop talking about it. He hung up his jacket, put his leather lunch box, stuffed with new scripts on his desk, and went into the kitchen to pour himself a drink. One he needed. He took a long pull. He was tired and he'd skipped lunch so his stomach was empty. The Scotch warmed him immediately. He took another pull, then refilled his glass, and went into the living room to sit down. Robbie was back at the window.

"Robbie, get away from there. Don't you have homework, or practice?"

Robbie's silence meant *yes*.

"Shouldn't you get on it? You're going to want to watch Rockford tonight."

"Sometimes I wish I was an ordinary kid."

Charlie frowned. "What do you mean by that?"

"If I didn't play I'd have a lot more time. Dad, can they arrest John?"

"I don't know. It depends upon what happened. Now go get busy. I'll see you at dinner."

Robbie went reluctantly, and Charlie sat looking at the pictures on the far wall. There were several reproductions and an original he'd bought years ago in the Village from Hammersmitt. Hammersmitt had ended his career on his big black BMW bike, on one of the curves along route 28, ten miles west of Woodstock. Charlie Hyatt had ended his career barricaded in his rent-controlled apartment on the upper westside.

Lynn came in with the chili powder. She paused, looking at him. "I see you've heard."

"What's happened now?"

Lynn knew little more than Robbie. A prowler, not a rapist, had gotten into the Wallace apartment and when John Mack encountered him in the fourth-floor hallway, the prowler had thrown a radio he was stealing at Mack and then gone for him with a knife. Mack had shot the man dead. The police had asked Mack to come down to the station to make a statement. No one thought he would be charged.

She ended by saying, "I never thought I'd see the day I'd be grateful that man was around."

"Nor so quickly, I'm sure," Charlie said with a particular emphasis.

She was sensitive to all his tones and she looked at him steadily as she asked, "What does that mean?"

"I'm not sure. Did anyone see what actually happened?"

"Yes, they did. Mr. Morrison was practically there. He told Ida and she told me. By the way, Ida wants to put together a little appreciation for Mack when he gets home."

"Oh, that's a wonderful idea."

Robbie began to warm up in the bedroom, playing whole notes in the bottom of the register. Lynn held up the chili powder and said, "I have to go give the stew some character," she said.

He followed Lynn into the kitchen to say, "Honey, I have a very strong bad feeling."

She turned with abrupt anger. "Well, so have I, when I think of someone loose in the halls with a knife. You know what happened to Fran. You know what can happen. Charlie, it's all around us."

"I know."

He put aside his apprehension until after dinner, and then he walked upstairs and rang Morrison's bell. Morrison was still eating and he asked Charlie in and tried to get him to have something. Charlie accepted a drink. They only had vodka, but he said he didn't care, as long as it had alcohol in it. Mrs. Morrison produced a serviceable screwdriver, but she didn't look like she enjoyed the job. Morrison sat hunched over the head of the table with a loaf of white bread. He smeared a slice from a margarine tub and ate out the soft white center, leaving the crust. His plate was lined with other crusts.

"That's right," he said to Charlie's first question, "I was practically on top of him when he dropped the guy. I was home so I was taking Bogart out early to get it over with, and Mack comes charging up the stairs like he's still playing commando, only he's serious. 'There's a prowler in the building,' he says. I hadn't seen anyone, but I put the dog back because I figured I'd better help him look. By the time I got Bogart inside, Mack was on up to the fourth floor. So I started after him, but halfway up I heard someone shout and then there was one shot that sounded like I was inside a big loud speaker. That's a loud sound, Mr. Hyatt.

"When I got up there, I found Mack kneeling in front of this guy, who had a hole right in the middle of his chest. 'He went for me,' Mack said, and he showed me the knife. It was an ugly thing, something someone had made out of a file."

Charlie sat up alertly.

"And the guy had also thrown a portable radio at Mack. That was there on the floor—"

"Wait a minute," Charlie broke in. "Tell me about this knife."

"It wasn't manufactured, if that's what you mean. It was homemade, out of a file I'd say, and it was pretty crude, but it looked sharp as shit." Morrison compressed his lips and shook his head. "I've seen a lot of knives, and this one was mean looking."

126

"Do you think this guy was in the Wallace apartment?"

"Sure, he had her stuff. The police checked all that. He went out the hall window and worked his way around the side of the building until he came to an unlatched window. It just happened to be Mrs. Wallace. Good thing she wasn't there."

"Morrison," Charlie said carefully, "we don't know each other, but we've been neighbors a while and that counts for something, so I want to ask you if there's anything about this that bothers you?"

Morrison frowned and smeared another slice of white bread with margarine. "Nah. He scorched that guy, it's true, but I wouldn't let no one come at me with a knife like that. Not when I'm carrying a gun. It's that simple to me, and, you know, Mrs. Wallace got her stuff back, some of it keepsakes from her husband, rest him, and the radio wasn't even broke." Morrison continued to watch Charlie as he ate the center out of his bread. "Why?" he asked, after he swallowed, "What does it mean to you?"

Again Charlies said, "I'm not sure." But when he left Morrison's he went on up to the fourth floor to look at the prowler's route into the Wallace apartment. The corridor window had been opened. There were streaks in the dust, and, looking out, he saw it was possible, just possible, to crawl around. A desperate man could do it. What other kind of man would launch himself into such a thoughtless venture?

Ida caught him on the way back and he had to hear the whole story again. Every time he heard it the prowler grew larger. Ida also told him she wanted to have coffee and cake for John Mack to show him how grateful they were. "He must feel awful," she said. "That poor man. He's the kindest thing when you get

127

to know him. You know the little park over by the edge of the river? Well, he sits with me there sometimes, so I can get a little air, and the other day he climbed a tree to put a baby bird back in its nest. It was something to see. That big man with that poor little thing in his hand."

When Charlie returned to his own apartment, Claire and Phil Julian were there. Neither of them had seen any of it. Phil had just phoned the police station to see if Mack needed any help, but everything was all right. He'd finished his statement and was on his way home. Lou Jacobs was going to wait for him at the front door and the rest of them were going to wait in the Jacobs' apartment.

After the Julians left, Lynn said, "I'm going up, and Robbie wants to go, too. I said it was all right. Are you coming?"

"No."

"Charlie, what's wrong?"

"Well, several things, if you want to know, but right now I don't think some poor junkie getting the shit shot out of him is any cause for celebration."

"No one's celebrating."

"Aren't they? Ida's as excited as if her son were coming home from the war, and Robbie acts like this asshole was the Lone Ranger."

"So that's it."

"No, that isn't it. Look, go on up, and take Robbie if you think it's all right."

She looked doubtful. "Are you going to be okay?"

"Sure. I've got something to do, anyway."

After they left, he made himself still another drink. He knew he was a little drunk, and maybe he needed to be still drunker. If he had a bee in his brain, the only thing to do was to free it and see where it flew.

He sat down to wait. In five minutes he heard foot-steps on the stairs, and then, from a distance, he heard the sound of applause. Applause! It was as crazy as cheering a gladiator. He sat thinking about what he was going to do.

But when he tried to get himself started, his nerve failed. Suppose it was nothing? Suppose Lynn was right, and he was simply reacting to his only half-conscious feeling that Mack was becoming the man of the house, the father of the whole damned building and everyone in it. He smiled at this realization, amused that he had fallen into such a cliché. John Mack was an employee, Charlie paid his salary, and that was the basic relationship. But was it? All right admit that, for the moment; something was still beginning to stink, and Charlie smelled it clearly. The best plan was to find out.

He let himself out of his apartment and cocked his ear at the stairwell to catch the sounds of the gathering on the fourth floor. He had waited too long, and now he had to hurry. Moving carefully in a manner he hadn't used since he was a boy, Charlie started into the basement. The short flight of steps was dark, and the only light was beyond, in the concrete corridor. The odors down here were strong and complex—gasoline and soap, paint and cleaning fluids. He noted Robbie's bike leaning against the wall, an odd shape in the shadows. He passed the laundry room, dark now, the white machines a luminous gray, and found the door to John Mack's office closed.

He turned the knob slowly—so slowly he had time to note how warm and greasy the metal felt—and stepped inside. The odor here was stale with the smell of tobacco, and the TV monitor with its picture of the empty lobby filled the room with a ghostly light. He switched on the overhead and went directly behind the desk. The main drawer was warped, and he had to jerk it sharply several times to get it open. The knife wasn't where it had been. He began to search the drawer, moving aside some lined note pads and a clutter of ballpoints. He was so intent that the footsteps were almost outside the door before he heard them. He put the desk in order, but the drawer wouldn't close.

Charlie was standing by the edge of the desk, looking into the monitor, when Mack came in. Mack was holding a large paper plate with several slices of cake. His face showed no surprise, and his eyes didn't flicker as he discovered Charlie.

"Can I help you with something, sir?"

"No," Charlie said, with as much ease as he could manage, "I like to watch this thing. People act very differently when they don't think anyone's watching them."

"You've noticed that, sir. I see some odd things on my little show there." Mack looked around and continued, in the same tone, "I don't think I left that drawer open."

"No, you didn't." Charlie produced a thin smile. "I was looking for something you showed me the other day."

"What was that, sir?"

"You called it a shank."

John Mack set the cake down on the desk, frowning in thought. Charlie was acutely aware of how powerful a man Mack seemed. A meat machine which moved with obvious efficiency. No fat there.

Mack turned to look at Charlie as he said, "Oh, yes, the day you were here with your son. I threw that thing away."

"Why?"

"What do you mean, sir?"

Charlie decided to push it. "I just don't get the feeling you're a man who would throw that kind of curio away. It's too much fun to show it to people. What happened here today, John?"

"You must have heard."

"I want to hear it from you."

Mack rested one hip on the desk and folded his arms. He smiled as he said, "Look, Mr. Hyatt, I just spent three hours talking to the crushers, and I'm about talked out."

Charlie decided not to yield. "Give it to me briefly."

"Okay. A prowler got in the building, tore up Mrs. Wallace's place, and when I caught him in the hall and called on him to surrender, he pitched a radio at me and came for me with a knife—"

"What kind of knife?"

"A shank, sir."

"Yes." Charlie began to take the final step. "A shank like the one you showed me, there in your desk. Now, doesn't that strike you as quite a coincidence?"

Mack shook his head calmly. "Not at all. There's hundreds of those things out there on the streets. They make them in the jails and bring them out with them. Shit, there's high-school kids making knives and zip guns in manual training. Now this man today was out on parole. They let him out of Green Meadows ninety days ago, and that's a real hard-rock warehouse up there. He probably carried that shank in Green Meadows and just went on carrying it out here. It would do the job, I can tell you that . . ."

John Mack fell silent, and Charlie continued to stare at him, unwilling to be pursuaded. Mack was very smooth and convincing, with every appearance

131

of candor, but once again Charlie sensed the combat sergeant who had learned to tell the officers only what he thought they needed to know.

As they stared at each other, a silent contest developed. Neither wanted to be the first to look away. After a long moment of this, Mack asked, "Is something bothering you, Mr. Hyatt?"

"Yes, John. Something's bothering me."

"Maybe if you could spell it out, I could put your mind at ease."

"When I can, I will."

Charlie's sense of theater told him he had just said his exit line. He stepped around Mack, heading for the door, ending the interview, but Mack wasn't finished. Behind his back, Charlie heard Mack say, "Any time, sir. You know where I am."

Charlie's face smarted as he went quickly upstairs. Mack had bested him, and he was ashamed of the relief he felt at being away from the man. He began to calm himself by remembering that John Mack was a man who killed other people. Had killed someone, some terrified sneak thief, just today. And the shank was gone. That was a fact.

Lynn was washing the dishes when he came in. He went in and stood beside her while he made himself another drink. "Where have you been?" she asked. "You don't look well."

He stared at her a moment, wondering whether to outline his suspicions and ask her opinion, but he decided to wait. "I stepped out for some air," he said.

She smiled. "Did they serve it in a glass?"

"No, I'm tired of Rosco's. It isn't the same anymore. The bars in the Village used to seem like our own living room, but Rosco's is just a place to drink."

"I've been wondering how long it would take you to figure that out."

Charlie didn't answer. He went back to the living room and began to work on the scripts he'd brought home. When she finished in the kitchen, Lynn came out and began to read. She was reading an account by a zoologist of his life among the great apes of Central Africa. Some woman had taught a captive gorilla to talk in sign language, and the creature had betrayed the intelligence of a dull-normal child. For some reason Charlie couldn't fathom why this fascinated Lynn. He went through one episode, doing some rewriting and the preliminary blocking, seeing in his mind how he would move the camera. He began another. Every time his attention wandered, he began to think about John Mack.

Robbie came out to watch *The Rockford Files*. When the program was over, it was his bedtime. That was the rule. Nor could he watch if his work wasn't done.

"Did you finish your homework?" Charlie asked.

Robbie nodded, without turning from the set. He was fine-tuning.

"How about practice?" Charlie went on. "I didn't hear you playing that much."

"I cut it a little short because of the party for John."

Charlie felt the urge to send Robbie back for another fifteen minutes on his clarinet, but he knew his impulse was mean, and he restrained himself. Why take it out on the kid? Robbie couldn't be expected to see through someone as subtle as John Mack. Rockford was on the screen, sprawled out with his feet on his small desk. Garner was a uniquely fine actor, a handsome man who had wisely decided not to depend on his looks. Charlie began to admire his work and was soon simply watching the show. Lynn watched, too, and Robbie lay spread out on the floor between them, with his chin in his hands. During commercial breaks they transacted their small business together. Lynn reminded Charlie to remember the cleaning. Robbie reminded both of them not to forget his concert.

It was the last commercial before Charlie began to wonder about John Mack. On the screen, Rockford/Garner had been working out a puzzle in detection, and Charlie realized he had been drawn into attempting the same thing. And that was crazy, because all these detective stories were trips, modern fantasies, while John Mack was just an ordinary man, a few-hundred-dollars-a-week security guard, who was earning his money the hard way. Charlie was building the crime of the century out of a few odd coincidences. He was at just the right stage of drunkenness to see things clearly, and he determined to get his mind off John Mack and onto something important.

When *The Rockford Files* was over, Robbie went to bed and Charlie made himself another drink. He walked into Robbie's room to ask him how the concert was shaping up. Robbie was putting on his pajamas, standing on one foot, swaying, while he tried to get his other foot into the flannel leg. "Pretty good. It's a little bogus."

"What isn't?" Charlie said with drunken good nature.

Robbie answered his smile. "Yeah. You know, Dad, sometimes I wish I'd taken trumpet."

"How's that?"

"It's more macho, I guess."

Charlie laughed. "Well, you could play sax."

"Nah, nobody wrote for it."

"That's a little different, isn't it?" Charlie said.

Robbie seemed to understand him, nodding his head seriously as he climbed into bed, and this pleased Charlie. One day soon he would be able to talk to Robbie just as he talked to Lynn, and it seemed miraculous that his child was becoming a human being right under his nose. He took a pull of his drink and looked around his son's private world with pleasure. Something on the bureau caught his notice. A dull lump of metal. He picked it up. It was heavy.

"What's this, Robbie?"

"A spent round."

"A what?"

"A bullet, Dad, one that's been fired."

"Where'd you get this?"

"From John, Mr. Mack, he said I could have it."

Charlie bounced the bullet on the palm of his hand. An ugly suspicion was forming in his mind. "Robbie, what sort of things does John Mack tell you?"

Robbie's face grew solemn. "Oh, nothing much, Dad, we just talk. He's interesting because he knows a lot of street stuff, about what's coming down out there . . ."

"Yes. Has he given you anything else?"

Robbie hesitated, then continued reluctantly, "Just a photo."

"Let me see it."

"Dad?" Robbie questioned this violation of his privacy.

"I want to see it. Now get it for me."

Robbie slipped out of bed and went to his dresser to open the top drawer. He pulled out a photo from out of a stack of his underwear and handed it to

Charlie. Charlie studied the picture with growing anger.

There were five members of an American rifle patrol and a prisoner. A Vietnamese stood stolidly, his arms bound behind him. He was little more than a boy, but his eyes were stoical. Four members of the plattoon were also kids, and the older man, the leader, was John Mack. Mack looked younger and even harder, a man at home in war, standing there in his crisp fatigues, wearing a helmet liner and a sidearm.

Charlie turned the photo over, and there, written with a black felt-tip pen, was:

> *To Robbie—*
> *Good luck and best wishes.*
> *—John*

Underneath the signature was a rudimentry flourish with two lines slashed across it. It was the self-satisfied exuberance of that ignorant schoolboy flourish that brought Charlie's anger to a boil.

He managed to speak to Robbie with calm sternness. "Robbie, I don't want you to hang around John Mack for a few days, until I tell you it's all right."

"Hey, Dad—"

Charlie let him go no further. "Rob, this is the red phone. Now do what I say."

He left, closing the door behind him, and found Lynn still reading. She held the book toward him, saying, "Look at this." He brushed it aside.

"No, you look at this."

He handed her the bullet and the photo. His hands were trembling. Her eyes widened as she put her book aside, but her reaction was to Charlie's emotion, rather than to the things he was pushing at her. She examined them briefly and asked, "But what do they mean to you?"

He began to rage. "That's a fucking bullet. John Mack gave it to Robbie. Look at it! It hit something soft. It was dug out of something, or somebody. And look at that photo. They got that poor bastard trussed up and he knows they're going to kill him. Look at it. Look at Mack. Like the fucking sheriff of Dodge City. This sucks. Giving this kind of shit to our kid. I don't trust that man. I think he's wrong in the worst way. I can smell it on him—"

Lynn broke in. "Honey, I don't smell anything like that."

"Goddammit, I know that. I can see. All right, listen to this—"

He began to outline all the peculiar evidence he thought was beginning to point to John Mack, and Lynn listened carefully until he came to the end and asked her, "All right, am I crazy?"

"I don't know. I really don't. But what can you do?"

"I can go to the police," he said simply. "And I can talk to McElroy and see what Mack was like over at his building. I was never quite sure why Mack left over there. I'm going to find out."

"That's what you have to do," Lynn said earnestly. "Find out what you can and then go to the police and let them judge the situation. They're professionals, Charlie."

He took the spent bullet and the photo of Mack and his squad and put them in his desk. He was certain these things were a message directed at him. He had asked Mack not to talk to Robbie about guns, and Mack had responded by giving Robbie a bullet. It was too obvious. In addition to the bullet, just to drive the point home, was a picture of the man who had fired it.

Charlie got into bed, adjusted the reading lamp, and tried to read, but he couldn't concentrate. He felt his home had been violated, and this awfulness wouldn't leave his mind. When Lynn came to bed, it became one of those rare nights when she just grinned at him and reached for his cock. He turned to her gratefully. A place to forget.

CHAPTER TWELVE

That night Charlie dreamed he was writing and directing a devastating documentary which proved everything was junk. With a calm and inexorable logic he exposed the essential junkiness of life's every aspect, and he woke without a shread of his argument intact, but still filled with some of the compassionate superiority of his dream self.

As he shaved, his mood lingered, and be began to review his evidence against John Mack. Clearly Lynn thought he was against Mack because he resented Mack's influence on Robbie. So, okay, say that's true. He did resent it. That still left a lot of ugly loose ends. He stared into his own eyes in the mirror, just as he stared into the eyes of strangers to judge their weight and sincerity, and he sensed how firmly he stood. At the same time and in a different part of his mind he noted the subtle signs announcing that he drank too much, ate too much, sat around too much.

He caught Robbie before he left for school and took his son by the upper arms, as he did when he was most serious. "I meant what I said last night, no more of this John Mack until I make sure he's all right."

Robbie met his eyes briefly, then looked away. "Dad, what have you got against John? Everyone likes him."

He saw how legitimate Robbie's question was. "I'm not sure, and I'll need a few days to find out. Trust me until then."

Lynn had turned to listen to their conversation. She was wearing her robe, her eyes still thickened with sleep. A flicker of displeasure crossed her face, but apparently she decided to say nothing. She waited until Charlie was finished before she told Robbie, "You put on a sweater. It's going to be cool today."

Robbie ran to obey, and Lynn turned to pour Charlie a cup of coffee. He sat down at the breakfast table and limited himself to one spoon of sugar. "Eggs?" Lynn asked.

"No, I've been eating too much. And I want to get going anyway, I've got to see McElroy, and after work I'm going to stop by the police station and talk to Lieutenant Yeager."

He knew Lynn made an effort to be reasonable, to see things as others saw them, but that effort wasn't easy this morning, when the sink was full of dirty dishes and he was off to play at Philip Marlowe. But he felt confident. He drank his coffee, kissed Lynn on the cheek with enough affection to bring back a little of the night, gathered his papers, and left. It was a cool morning, and the city was as fresh as it ever is. He walked over to the subway stop with a quick step. From across the street he saw three black boys lounging against the iron fence that guarded the subway entrance. They were laughing and slapping each other's palms. Their white teeth flashed in self-satisfied good nature.

Charlie tightened. An encounter was always possible. Twelve people had been killed in the subways in the last six months. Twelve people who had started out as passengers and ended as victims. Three of them had been pushed in front of oncoming trains; their bodies had had to be collected in bags. Others had been knifed. Two had been shot.

As he crossed the street, Charlie saw the boys were young, twelve or thirteen, filled with simple high spirits. He now saw their books and knew they were on their way to school, and he was disappointed at how instinctively he had become alarmed. If they had been white he would have hardly noticed them, but three black boys were immediately a gang and potentially dangerous. They didn't even notice Charlie as he ducked down the stairs. One more middle-aged paddy on his way to sit in an office and make marks on pieces of paper.

The subway was an underworld of white tile and gray I-beams filled with a cold and even light, the same at midnight as it was at noon, and Charlie passed through it, standing on the platform, standing on the swaying train, in a mood of passive suspension. All those in the crowded car seemed to share his mood. No one talked, few read, most simply stared and waited for the ride to end. Every smooth surface was densely spray-painted and inked with felt markers. He got off at Rockefeller Center and took the elevator to the thirty-sixth floor, where he stepped into a deeply carpeted hallway where a young and pretty girl sat behind a small white desk.

"Good morning, Mr. Hyatt," she said.

"Yes, thanks. Mr. McElroy's expecting me."

"Oh, I don't think he's in."

She said nothing more, but looked back at something she was writing. "Is he running late?" Charlie asked.

"I don't think he's coming in today." She stared at him pensively. She knew Charlie was important, but she wasn't certain how important. "Do you want to see his secretary?"

"I sure do."

Mary Lou Gellers told him McElroy was sick. "He's got some stomach thing that's been going around."

"Is he in the city?"

"No, I think he went out to the Island. Is it something important?"

"Well, it's private, really. I'll see if I can get him on the phone."

Charlie went to his own office and placed a call to McElroy at his Long Island number. When McElroy came on, his voice was tired. "Hello, Charlie, what's wrong?"

"Look, I'm sorry to bother you, but I seem to have a bear by the tail. Do you remember that John Mack character you steered to us?"

There was a pause on the other end, then "Oh, yes, the security man."

Charlie chose his words carefully. "What was he like when he was working for you?"

142

"Very efficient."

"But were there any . . . incidents?"

"Charlie, can this wait? I'm not feeling well . . ." Again he paused. "I'll talk to you in the next day or two."

Charlie couldn't let go. "Is there something I should know?"

When McElroy spoke again, his voice had grown distant. "I'll talk to you when I get back." There was also that veiled hint men in authority learn to use— the hint was to remind Charlie that everything good in his life came to him through McElroy.

Charlie hung up, more anxious now. Wasn't it clear there was something McElroy didn't want to tell him? But why? The man was simply sick. And so was Charlie. Charlie was catching an *idée fixe,* which had caused him to badger his boss. Let it go, old sport, he counseled himself. He sat staring at a framed playbill. One of his Village exercises. If the devil appeared to offer him his illusions back, would he strike the deal?

Then someone came in to bring him the first problem of the day. A walk-on he'd hired through SAG was sick and he needed a replacement immediately. His secretary could do it—hell, the cleaning woman could do it—but, no, it had to be a SAG member. He reached for the phone.

Later that afternoon, he telephoned Lieutenant Yeager and made an appointment to see him at five o'clock.

He had to wait for Yeager. It didn't surprise him. All these city services, which looked so fine on paper, broke down in practice, and you and your problem became part of the process. Everyone waited, even the powerful, and if you were poor you simply waited

143

longer. Charlie settled on one end of a bench, and two large black women sat on the other. Across the narrow aisle, there was a boy wearing only a pair of pants. His feet were bare, and he folded his arms over his naked chest. Here and there along the worn green linoleum sat number 10 cans, each with a few inches of stained brown water. Cigarette butts floated on the surface. At the end of the corridor there was a large white clock with a red second hand. When Charlie sat down it was four minutes to five.

At 5:15, a uniformed policeman came and handed the boy a collarless white shirt, the kind worn by hospital orderlies and dishwashers, and stood waiting while he put it on. Charlie stared at the boy as if he were an actor reading for a part, working through some silent business, but then their eyes met, and Charlie saw a curious combination of misery and angry hostility. At 5:22, the two black women stood up and left. A Hispanic man came and sat down in their place. He wore a cheap suit, cut to extreme fashion, and carried a plastic briefcase.

At 5:38, Yeager finally came by. He seemed to be wearing the same clothes, and he was in a hurry. "What can I do for you, Mr. Hyatt?"

The forty minutes he had spent cooling his heels had taken some of the steam out of Charlie. "There was a shooting in my building yesterday."

"That's right," Yeager said, as if Charlie had asked a question. "An SD."

Charlie stood up. He was taller than Yeager, and he used his height to look down at the detective. "I want to see the file."

"What's your interest?"

Charlie said evenly, "In the past month two men

have been killed within a hundred feet of my door. That's my interest."

Yeager tried to look sympathetic. "I'm not supposed to let you see our reports."

Charlie shook his head. "That isn't what I mean. I want to see the shank."

"Come on, give me a break, Mr. Hyatt, what are you talking about?"

"The man who was shot and killed yesterday was supposed to be armed with a homemade knife, made out of a file. That's what I want to see."

Yeager nodded. "Okay, now you want to tell me why?"

"Yes, I'd be glad to. Because I saw a similar knife in Mr. Mack's desk several days before. It's Mack and only Mack who says the man he shot was armed. If the knife taken out of that man's hand turned out to be the same knife I saw in John Mack's desk . . ."

Charlie deliberately left the implication in the air, and Yeager stared up at him intently until he was sure Charlie meant what he was saying. Then the detective nodded briskly and said, "Okay, come on back and let's take a look."

Yeager led him into a squad room, and Charlie immediately noted that it was less colorful than the sets used on the cop shows. A detective in a sober suit sat using the phone—he could just as easily have been an insurance salesman working a client—while another in a white shirt and a red sweater vest typed in rapid bursts. Yeager sat Charlie beside his own desk as he said, "I'll be right back."

Charlie waited, studying the bulletin board next to the door. It displayed a dense panel of wanted posters and duty rosters. The wanted men stared out into the room, and they all looked the same. The detective in the suit hung up. Noticing Charlie, he stared at him for a moment before he folded a small notebook and put it carefully into his inside pocket.

Yeager came back with a large manila envelope and a plastic folder. He put the folder on his desk and opened the envelope. He drew out a knife and held it so Charlie could study it. Charlie's first feeling was one of misgiving. He had expected it would be easy to say it either was or wasn't the knife he had seen in Mack's desk, but now that he was looking at it, he realized he couldn't be sure. The knife in front of him was obviously a file, but the workmanship seemed more finished. The point looked sharper, the edge more finely ground, and the handle more carefully wrapped.

"Do you see a lot of these things?" he asked Yeager.

"No, this is a real curiosity. Is this the shank you saw?"

"I'm not sure."

Yeager put the knife back in the evidence envelope and sat down. He opened the folder and read for a while; then he looked up and said, "I don't see anything here, Mr. Hyatt. The victim was a convicted criminal with an extensive record, out on parole, caught red-handed. He knew he was going back to the joint, dead bang, and he was desperate enough to try to cut his way out."

"Was he a junkie?"

"Probably."

"Drug addicts don't usually carry weapons, do they?"

A look of amusement crossed Yeager's face. "Did you read that in the *Times*, Mr. Hyatt?"

"Suppose I did, does that mean it's not true?"

Yeager swung around in his chair and touched

Charlie lightly on the knee. "Listen, Mr. Hyatt, a lot of different kinds of men catch habits for a lot of different reasons. Three's no typical addict any more than there's a typical cop. Now what's bothering you? Are you suggesting this Mack's trigger-happy?"

"That's about it. I thnk he's a very dangerous and devious man."

"Look, Mr. Hyatt, suppose a burglar came at you with a knife, what would you do?"

"I can't imagine."

"Well, isn't that it? Maybe you'd try to disarm him without shooting, and maybe you wouldn't."

"It's the knife that bothers me. You say it's a curiosity, but Mack says every asshole on the street has one. He says they make them in the prisons and bring them out with them."

Yeager shook his head. "He's putting you on. Why would some con want to smuggle out his shank when any punk can buy a switchblade for five dollars?"

Charlie leaned forward eagerly. "But I'm supposed to have seen *two* of them in the last few days."

"I know—"

Charlie rushed on. "There's been a lot of other stuff before this. Nothing definite, but it all adds up to something heavy." He began to trace the various odd connections, carefully building his case. Yeager listened impassively, but before he could respond he was called away. The police report was left open on the desk. After a moment's hesitation, during which he reminded himself that his taxes helped pay for this whole show, Charlie pulled the report over to where he could read it. He was impressed with the detail. Somehow he'd formed the impression the cops were slipshod. They weren't. The man who up to now had been either the Junkie or the Victim had a name—Anthony Flores; he had a mother, a father, two brothers, both younger; and he had left a record of his life. Charlie saw a mug shot, probably taken at sixteen, and another at twenty-two, and still another at thirty-one. The change was cruel. How quickly Anthony Flores's luck had run out. The final picture was an eight-by-ten of the corpse, fallen in the hallway. The shank was clearly visible lying beside the dead man's hand, and it had been circled with a grease pencil.

Something about the knife in the photo tugged at him, and he opened the manila envelope to look at the real knife again. It was an ugly thing, both heavier and colder than it looked. Suddenly he realized that this file was the same brand as the one Mack had shown him. He saw the distinctive trademark. What it most looked like was the same knife with more work done on it. A better workman trying to smooth out the crudeness.

He replaced the knife and returned to the record. Reading swiftly, he went through the officer's report and follow-up. He came to something that brought a cold chill through him, and he was still adjusting to this new information when Yeager came back. "Those files are confidential," the detective said with official coldness.

Charlie stood his ground. "I see why. You weren't going to tell me this is Mack's second killing, were you?"

"That was four years ago, and if you read it carefully you'll see where Mack had witnesses, *two* witnesses, that the intruder pulled a gun. We found that gun—"

"Just like you found a knife. And what about all that other stuff I told you?"

Yeager took his seat, shaking his head. "You told it well, that's all, you made it interesting, and I like detective stories myself, but they're all a bunch of shit, even the ones that are supposed to be real. Let me tell you something they leave out. Two or three people like Tony Flores go down every week around here. If not one way, another. If they don't total a car or take an overdose, they force some cop to shoot them. That's the reality, Mr. Hyatt, they go down all the time, and we got a good enough story on this one to let it go. Well, don't look so shocked, what did you think was going on? I'll tell you something else . . ."

Yeager looked directly into Charlie's eyes. "You got a very good man there. John Mack is professional, and he's got a mean rep all over the West Side. The street element knows who he is and they're afraid of him—"

Charlie broke in to say, "So am I."

"Maybe you're afraid of the wrong person. Now, I can't give this any more time, do you want to make a formal complaint?"

"Will it do any good?"

"Frankly, probably not."

"May I borrow that knife for a day or two?"

"Mr. Hyatt, cut that shit out."

Charlie stood up and looked down at Yeager. "Sure, why not? He was only a scumbag, right? Just let it go."

Charlie walked off and found his own way out.

CHAPTER THIRTEEN

Charlie was still mad when he reached home, and he caught Lynn in the kitchen and began to rage at her about the other dead man, four years before. Then, unable to stop himself, he repeated the whole chain of evidence he had recited to Yeager and recited to her before, pointing out and underlining, but gradually he grew calm enough to realize she was handling him carefully.

He paused, and then went on in a quieter and more reasonable tone. "Don't you see, John Mack kills people and gets away with it because his stories are good enough and the people don't matter anyway. That's really evil."

Lynn turned to face him, and he saw that her eyes were troubled: "Charlie, this isn't a good subject for us. If we talk about it, we'll just end up quarreling, and we don't need that on top of everything else. You do what you think you should do."

"I will. I'm going to call a tenants' meeting. Everyone else should know what I know, and you know what I think's going to happen? I think they're going to vote that monster right out of this building."

"You talk like he was Hitler."

"You're damn right I do. You think Hitler was so special? He just had more opportunities and better technology."

Charlie heard Robbie's step in the hallway, and he dropped the conversation and turned to begin a drink. Robbie looked in with his nice wise-kid smile. "You two yelling again?" he asked.

"Just practicing," Charlie said. "Are you up for tonight?"

Lynn noted the size of the drink Charlie was pouring and said automatically, "You're the one who's going to be up."

Robbie chose to shrug. One moment the concert was important, the next it wasn't. "I warmed up for an hour," he said, "after I came home from school. I only got one decent reed, so I have to baby that, because if it blows I'm fucked—"

"Robbie!" Lynn said.

"Oh, Mom, I don't mean anything by that."

Charlie said to Lynn, "Are you trying to preserve the pure meaning of that overused word"—he heard his tone growing sarcastic—"or are you afraid he'll use it in front of Ida Jacobs and she'll blame you because you're a bad mommy?"

"Okay, Charlie, why don't you just drink your drink."

"I will."

Charlie went into the living room, and found the family phone book in a pile of old magazines. He sat down, putting his drink on a table beside his chair, noting for a moment all the rings left from the glasses he had set there, and then he picked up the phone and began to call the other tenants. Phil Julian was at the hospital, but he told Claire, and then he caught Chambers. Chambers listened quietly and then agreed it was something they needed to talk over.

Charlie asked, "Can I use your name when I talk to the others? Just to say you agree?"

Chambers didn't answer immediately, and Charlie heard a faint whisper of music, sucked somehow into the phone line, and then Chambers was saying, "Yes, that's okay."

Charlie went on drinking—he was too wound up and he needed it—but he took a shower and put on some clothes that he thought looked good. He knew this was important to Robbie. Lynn also took the trouble to dress up. She wore velveteen jeans and Annie Oakley boots, and brushed her hair until it was smooth and shiny. She had once overheard Robbie and two of his friends discussing the mother of another friend who wasn't with them, and she had never forgotten the casual and savage sophistication with which they had characterized her appearance. Robbie came out of his room wearing his band suit, carrying his horn case, smiling with suppressed pride.

Charlie thought: How handsome he is. How handsome he will be. And he filled with pride himself. Lynn just smiled at her son, before she bent to kiss him gravely on the cheek. It was one of those moments that fed the family, and Charlie made a conscious decision to put aside the John Mack problem for the rest of the night.

They walked over to the school auditorium, six short blocks, and it was one of those nights when the city seemed cool and friendly. A breeze blew off the Hudson, and everyone seemed to be enjoying it. On some streets people sat on the stoops, whole families, some with both grown children and new babies, and in the open windows on the second and third floor the old people were sitting. The Tony Floreses came from such families. Any one of those little boys might grow up to end the same.

They passed a small bar with neon beer signs lit in its opaque windows, and Charlie tried to imagine he could run in for a fast hit and then catch up with Lynn and Robbie, but he knew how they would see it. They would think he couldn't go half an hour without a drink. He began to think ahead. Maybe he could slip out of the concert and walk back for a couple. That was gross.

At the auditorium, Robbie went down the side aisle and behind the stage, while he and Lynn looked for seats. They found a still-open row halfway back on the left side and took the two on the aisle. Up on the stage the music stands were lined up in rows. Several kids were already seated and warming up.

Gradually the stage filled. He watched Robbie walk on, noting how tall he was. Robbie took his seat in the first row and began to assemble his clarinet. Every kid on the stage was noodling, and many of them were practicing licks they wouldn't be playing, taking this unscheduled moment to strut what they thought was their stuff. It amounted to fifty simultaneous solos, and Charlie began to find it unnerving. He should have gone for a drink immediately. He could have been back by now. He glanced at his watch.

Lynn reached over to take his hand, and he began to try to calm himself down. The teacher/conductor walked onstage, and Charlie joined in the polite applause for this man who listed himself in the program as "E. Donald Tyler." Tyler signaled the oboe to give the concert A, and the band began to tune up. Charlie watched Robbie, pleased at how professional his son seemed. The overture was brisk, and Charlie found himself enjoying the music. He looked around, trying to get some feel of the audience, and he saw many of the parents he always saw at these concerts. A large part of the audience was family. Suddenly, he stiffened.

Sitting across the aisle and about five seats back was John Mack. He wore his same gray suit; his hat was on his lap. Charlie had the distinct impression Mack had been staring at him. Their eyes locked for a moment. Then Mack smiled and nodded, gesturing at Robbie up on the stage, and he jerked both thumbs up in front of his chest to say Robbie was A-1. Charlie turned away. To him the congratulatory gesture had been filled with stale military theater.

Charlie's first thought was that Robbie had disobeyed him. Then he realized Robbie had been talking about this concert for several weeks and in that time he had undoubtedly invited John Mack. Charlie could understand that. But he couldn't understand why Mack was here. What was a streetwise professional soldier doing in a grade-school auditorium? Charlie began to remember how Phil Julian had had a little

superior fun with John Mack the night Mack had issued their keys, and a few nights later Julian's apartment was torn up.

Lynn bent toward him to whisper, "What's the matter with you?"

Charlie put his mouth close to her ear. "Mack's
here."

"What?"

A woman in front turned around to look at them.
Charlie took Lynn's hand firmly and shook his head.
The concert was ruined for him. He scarcely heard
the rest of the program. The medley from *Hello,
Dolly* was half over before he remembered Robbie
was supposed to have a solo, and even when Robbie
stood up with three other boys to play a dixieland
chorus, he still had trouble concentrating. He was
thinking how he would get Lynn and Robbie out of
here without having to encounter John Mack. He ad-
mitted to himself he was afraid, and he assured himself his fear was normal. He'd fight this bastard in his
own way.

The moment the final applause ended, after three
bows, Charlie took Lynn firmly by the arms and
started toward the stage. Lynn began to complain,
but he cut her off, saying, "I'll explain later." They
found Robbie behind the curtain in the wings, cleaning his horn before he put it away. "Let that go," he
told Robbie. "Come on, we're in a hurry." Robbie shot
him a quick glance, read his father's expression, and
began to obey. Charlie was sure Mack would follow
them. Mack would want the encounter so he could go
on playing his game. Even after Charlie had hustled
his family out the side door, he searched the streets
carefully to make sure Mack was nowhere around.

"Are you going to tell me what that was all about?"

Lynn asked. "And are you going to say a word to your son about his solo?"

"Robbie, I'm sorry."

Robbie didn't answer.

"You played very well," Charlie said, aware of how false he sounded.

"Thanks," Robbie said tightly, and continued to walk ahead of them without looking back.

"Well," Lynn said, "that's Robbie out of the way. What about me?"

"I can't talk about it right now."

Robbie went to his room immediately. He didn't say good night. Charlie went to the kitchen to pour a drink. "I'll take one of those," Lynn said. When he handed her a Scotch, Lynn went on, "You know you've hurt him?"

"I know that. Look, I'll fix it. John Mack was there. He was about five rows behind us."

"Charlie, listen to me." Lynn put her hand on his arm. Her fingertips were cool from the ice in her glass. "You're letting this thing make you a little crazy."

Charlie covered her hand with his own. "No, I don't think so. Something's wrong."

"But I know you, baby, and when you get going on something your judgment's not always that good."

He stepped away. "This is different. And it's not for us to decide. I just happened to see a few things that put me to thinking about this asshole, and it's clear to me everyone has a right to know what I saw so they can make their own decision about what it means. Now I put it to you, that's not crazy."

She saw his reason and was silent for a moment. Then her expression changed as she said, "Well, my truth is, Charlie, I feel a lot safer with that man down

157

in the basement. He's very cordial, and several times he's helped me with the groceries—"

"Lynn! That's his game."

Charlie walked into the living room and made the rest of the calls. Everyone agreed to meet the following evening in Charlie's apartment. When he had worked his way through the list, he realized that Lynn had gone to bed. He walked into their bedroom to see if she was reading, but her light was out and she was already curled in the position she used to fall asleep.

Neither his son nor his wife had bothered to say good night to him. A momentary sadness passed through him. He looked at his wife, who had deliberately removed herself, and considered how he was being judged by his culture. In the kitchen, he poured himself another drink. He made it straight, and opened a bottle of beer to wash it with. He caught the tail of the eleven o'clock news on ABC and then switched to Channel 5 for *Charlie Chan at the Circus*. He had several more large drinks, and only during the increasingly longer and more frequent commercial breaks did he think about the meeting tomorrow and what he would say.

CHAPTER FOURTEEN

Charlie woke just as the windows were beginning to stain with a cold gray light. He had passed out in the chair. The TV was still on. The tube glowed with a spectral light, and the low, uneven hum filled the room with its implications of waste and disorder. Charlie's first thought was: Not again. Why could he never remember at night how he would feel in the morning?

He switched off the box and took his empty glass into the kitchen. The stale smell of Scotch intensified his sickness. He drank two glasses of cold water and went into the bathroom to take a brisk shower. Afterward, he brushed his teeth and settled into his usual place beside Lynn. She turned, opened her eyes, looked at him briefly, then closed her eyes again. Perversely, he was horny. He moved nearer to her and tried to fondle her, but she wasn't having any. She turned away and said, "You're going to have to handle that by yourself."

"I never tell you that."

"Yes you have, lots of times. Now let me sleep."

Charlie didn't expect to sleep. He could never sleep when he wanted it the most, and he lay awake for an hour, thinking about himself and wondering at the process which had brought him here to this place, to this bed, with this hangover. Then he did sleep. And woke again at nine-thirty.

He took another shower and made himself some instant coffee. He saw the remains of Robbie's breakfast, half a bowl of milk with cornflakes floating in it, sitting in the sink. Robbie was stretched out in front of the TV, watching cartoons. Charlie sat down on the couch, balancing his coffee, and began to watch a mouse beating up on a cat.

"Where's your mother?" he asked.

"She's doing laundry," Robbie said, without taking his eyes off the set.

"I'm sorry about last night."

Robbie didn't answer.

Charlie went on, picking his words carefully. "I know you think I'm acting like an asshole, but I'm trying to act like a parent, and that's not always the easiest job in the world."

Now Robbie turned to look at him, and his expression was untroubled. "It's okay, Dad. I'm not brooding about it."

Charlie could have accepted this, but he was

wound up with a welter of emotions. "I don't mean to lay an old saw on you, and I want you to know I think you're loaded with honest good sense, but there really are things you will understand better when you're older."

"I believe you. Dad, can I go to the show this afternoon?"

Charlie felt a flow of relief, and for a moment he forgot his head. Smiling at Robbie, he said, "Sure. What're you going to see?"

"Oh, there's a double horror show up on Ninety-sixth. Jonathon, Eric, and I are going."

When Lynn came back, she was neutral, and Charlie decided not to push it. The meeting would tell everything, and until then it was better left alone. He didn't want John Mack in his apartment. That was the very thing that angered him the most. He deliberately put Mack out of his mind and settled down at his desk to do some work. Bills to pay, letters that had to be answered. All the paper shadows of his life. He began to think of an archivist a thousand years from now carefully studying these written transactions that were crossing his desk, just as contemporary scholars pored over the household accounts of Sumerian citizens, and the thought amused him. He played with it as he worked, and so when he heard John Mack's voice at his own door it was a moment before he recognized it.

A shock went through Charlie.

Mack was telling Lynn that he had seen her in a commercial the night before. Charlie sat listening.

"You could have driven a truck into my mouth. It just popped open. There you were right on the screen. I didn't know you were an actress."

Then he heard Lynn say, "I'm not, really. I used to

want to be an actress, but I gave it up when Robbie came."

"Begging your pardon, ma'am, but what I saw on that tube was an actress. You made me want one of those cakes."

"Well, thank you, John. Was there something else?"

"Yes, ma'am, I'd like to talk to your husband, if he's in."

"Let me see what he's doing."

Charlie waited for Lynn to come in. He felt very alert. Lynn appeared, her expression careful. "John Mack's here," she said. "He wants to see you."

"I know. Ask him to come in."

Charlie had decided to stay behind his desk. John Mack came in with his hat in his hand, looking around. "You've got this place fixed up real nice. Not like some of these units."

"We like it."

Charlie didn't rise, or offer his hand, and Mack ended up standing in front of his desk, which was what Charlie had intended.

"I was just telling your wife I saw her on a commercial . . ."

"Yes, I heard that."

Charlie stared up at Mack, giving him no help, forcing him to come to the point.

Mack looked calm and his eyes were quiet, but Charlie thought he knew what it meant when Mack laid his hat on Charlie's desk. Near the edge, but still on Charlie's desk. Jesus, the bastard was subtle. He'd trumped Charlie's behind-the-desk ploy, neatly and casually, and his voice was smooth as he said, "I heard you were getting the tenants together tonight."

"You heard right."

"I was just wondering if it's anything I should know about?"

"You'll hear about it soon enough. I'm going to ask them to terminate your services."

"I don't understand."

"I think you do."

"No, sir, I—"

Charlie cut him off. "Understand this—I want you out of here."

For a moment Mack's composure slipped, and Charlie thought he saw a hard flash in Mack's eyes. Then Mack shifted into the at-ease posture, legs slightly spread, hands clasped behind his back, his shoulders squared. When he began to speak, his eyes were focused about six inches above Charlie's head.

"I know you haven't been too happy with my work, and I don't understand that, because I asked you to pin it down for me so I could work on it, I asked you for specifics—"

"If you want specifics, come to the meeting."

"I can't, sir, I'm taking off tonight, and even if I weren't, I don't think I should be there. But if you've got something against me, I think you should tell me now."

Again Charlie thought he saw how Mack must have dealt with officers in the Corps. Mack would have been one of those NCOs who saw officers as his natural enemy, and he had learned to walk the line with them. Always pushing, always careful not to push too much.

"If you want to hear what I have to say, you come to the meeting. I don't deny you the right to defend yourself."

"Well, thank you, sir. Is it the photo?"

"No, it isn't. I don't like that picture one bit, but that isn't it."

"Robbie asked me for a snapshot, and it was the only one I had. Personally, I was kind of proud of that picture, but I can see how someone like you might not like it."

"I don't want to talk about this. Now, I have some calls to make."

Charlie couldn't say "Sergeant, you're dismissed," but he had found the equivalent. For a moment Mack lowered his eyes to meet Charlie's, and again Charlie saw a hard, flinty look.

"You're making a mistake, Mr. Hyatt. I know you don't think so, but you are."

Charlie didn't answer, and after a moment longer, Mack picked up his hat, put it on his head, and walked out. Charlie waited until he heard his front door close, and then he got up and went to find Lynn. She was in the bedroom, folding the fresh laundry.

"Did you hear that?" he demanded.

She didn't pause in her work. "I wasn't listening."

"Mack as much as threatened me. He told me I was making a mistake. Now what's that supposed to mean?"

"Charlie, stop and think. You're after his job. How would you react if someone was after your job?"

After the incident with Mack, the day began to take on an unreal quality. Charlie's hangover persisted. His head ached, his stomach was uneasy, and his teeth felt covered with moss. He struggled with a feeling of uselessness, as if he were stunted, incompetent, and he was morbidly conscious of the smells around him. Particularly on the street. Early in the afternoon he had convinced himself it would be all right to go over to Rosco's for a couple of ice-cold beers. They frosted the glasses in a cold locker and served them up still steaming.

The beer went down his throat like a radiant medicine, and he was actually able to call a halt at just two, and start back home. Outside, the smells and the shrill noises of the street began to eat away at his cure, and once again he began to worry that he wouldn't be convincing at the meeting tonight. He had to make them see what he saw.

Ahead of him, Jonathon and Eric, Robbie's friends, cut across the street. Jonathon saw him and smiled.

"How are you, Mr. Hyatt?"

"Okay. You back from the show?"

"Yeah. They weren't that scary."

"Where's Robbie?" Charlie asked.

"Oh, he ran into someone just as we were starting out, and he decided to go with them instead."

"What do you mean?"

Jonathon looked puzzled. "Nothing, he just ran into a friend."

"What friend?" Charlie asked.

"Your security guard, John, he had something cooked up for them to do."

Charlie stopped, and Jonathon went on a few steps before stopping himself. "What's the matter, Mr. Hyatt?"

"Do you know where they went?"

"No, I'm afraid I don't."

Charlie hurried back to the building and went down into the basement. In Mack's office he found a heavyset young man with thick glasses sitting at Mack's desk, watching the monitor.

"Where's Mack?"

"He's taking the rest of the day off."

"Do you know where he went?"

"No. Can I help you? I'm baby-sitting."

"This is personal. Do you have his number and his address out in Queens?"

"Yes, sir."

Charlie copied the information and ran up the stairs. Even before he talked to Lynn, he tried Mack's number, but there was no answer. Charlie had been almost certain Mack wouldn't be answering his phone. Next he dialed the police, but hung up after the first ring. Again he had nothing definite. Dealing with Mack was like dealing with a shadow. Every time Charlie looked at the shadow it seemed to have more substance, and yet it still would not quite take form. Whatever Mack and Robbie were off doing, Mack would take care to see that it looked innocent. Innocent to everyone but Charlie.

He found Lynn reading an old copy of *The New Yorker.* "Now that motherfucker's off with our kid."

She stared at him over the top of the magazine. "What do you mean?"

"Robbie's gone somewhere with John Mack. I heard it from Jonathon. Robbie didn't go to the show with them. Mack's taken him somewhere. He's warning me. Don't you see that? And Robbie disobeyed me, on top of everything else."

Lynn's expression grew serious. "Where do you think they might be?"

"How the fuck should I know? I'll go out and look around."

Charlie covered the entire neighborhood. He looked in the pool halls and the ping-pong palaces, and the penny arcade. He walked along the park that bordered the river, and stopped by the school. Every time he saw a kid of Robbie's height and coloring, his heart began to pound. He knew if he found Mack and

Robbie together he would end up fighting Mack. He was that angry.

Finally, he tired and headed back home. As soon as he was in the apartment, Lynn called, "Did you find him?"

Charlie closed the door and automatically bolted it. "No. I looked everywhere I could think of."

"Oh, I wish you'd never got this started."

Charlie was shocked at her tone, and went directly to the kitchen to make himself a drink. He'd waited for it long enough. But when he had the drink in front of him, he decided against it. He would need a clear head. Mack was fighting back, but Charlie knew he was in the right, and he wasn't going to give up.

But as afternoon wore into evening, Lynn grew more and more nervous, and finally Charlie called the station again. This time he asked for Lieutenant Yeager, but Yeager was off duty, and the desk sergeant wouldn't give Charlie the lieutenant's home number. He hung up. Yeager was the only one over there who might grasp the situation.

He walked into the living room, where Lynn was sitting staring at the windows. "I don't know," he said.

Lynn spoke without turning. "It's getting dark."

CHAPTER FIFTEEN

Charlie was convinced John Mack was warped. The question that bothered him as the evening wore away was, Just how warped? Was he crazy enough to hurt Robbie? Charlie didn't think so—Mack was very careful, and there were witnesses who had seen Robbie go off with Mack—but he couldn't be sure. His son had gone off to watch play monsters and ended up with a real one.

Charlie was so anxious about Robbie that it was 8:15 before he noticed that no one was showing up for the meeting. That was unusual. The Julians in particular had formed the habit of coming a little early for a drink and some jokes. He ran downstairs to see them. Claire answered the door, looking out around the chain. She smiled when she saw him. "Charlie, come on in. Settle an argument."

He entered the apartment and saw Phil Julian sitting in front of the television, in his bathrobe. Behind him Claire went on, "We're having a fight. I want to watch junk, and Phil insists we have to watch Channel Thirteen. They have a special on the migratory habits of the sea otter—"

"Bail us out," Phil said. "We need a referee."

Charlie stared, dumbfounded. "What are you doing here? You're supposed to be at my place."

"The meeting?" Phil asked.

"Yes, the meeting."

"Why, John Mack said it was canceled. He said you and he had talked and decided a meeting wasn't necessary."

"That tears it," Charlie said. "Get dressed and come on up. I'll get the others."

"Now wait a minute," Phil said, reacting to Charlie's tone.

"Phil, back me on this. This is serious. The bastard's got Robbie. And I didn't agree there wasn't going to be a meeting. Mack canceled it on his own, and then he went out and found my son, and I don't know where they've gone."

Julian stared up at Charlie. Then he said, "Okay, okay, we'll be right up."

When Charlie was finished running up and down the halls, he had collected fewer than half the tenants. The Chamberses were out, and that bothered him because he had depended on their quiet good sense. It was a small group he found himself addressing, and soon as they found out he wanted to fire John Mack, they were mostly against him.

"Let me trace it back for you," he said earnestly, looking at Ida Jacobs, who seemed the most distressed. "I was for Mack, you know, I wanted him in here, and I wasn't annoyed by all his excessive security, like some of you. But then I began to see things. One night I was out for a drink and I saw Mack on the corner wtih a superfly type, who really matched Fran's description of the man who attacked her. I didn't think too much of it at the time, because there's more than one shaved head in New York, but after some other things happened, I began to wonder. It was the attack on Fran that caused us to bring John Mack to work here. What if he arranged the attack—"

He saw total disbelief on Ida Jacobs's face, and Fran Jeffries looked miserable. He hurried on. "I have reason to think John Mack wanted this job more than he let on."

"Do you know that for sure?" Phil Julian asked.

"No, I don't, but I'm pretty sure. Let me go on. The next thing that happened was the burglary. Mack told us the burglars ran out the front door, but Rudy Simbro was sitting in the newsstand just across the street the whole evening and he never saw anyone come out. Mack saw me talking to Rudy, and the next night Rudy was beaten so badly he's still in the hospital. And he's afraid to say anything. The odd thing about the burglary was that nothing was taken. The apartment was trashed, that's all."

Again Julian interrupted. "But John surprised the burglars. They dropped everything and ran."

"Do you believe that?" Charlie demanded. "Do you really think he came through that window? I don't.

That man has huge shoulders and a forty-eight-inch chest, and there's no way he came through that window."

"Then how'd he get in?" Morrison asked.

"Through the door. He walked in the door with one of those keys he had made, and he trashed that apartment. He broke those bars out from inside and made up a story about surprising two thieves."

Ida Jacobs spoke up. "Mr. Hyatt, why would he do that?"

"To make himself seem necessary and to punish Dr. Julian for not taking him seriously. Ida, we're dealing with a strange man. He was in the service for many years. He was a noncomissioned officer, and I think he must have learned to hate his superiors. To Mack, Dr. Julian was an officer, and Mack punished him. He's punishing me right now. He's taken Robbie somewhere, and this is a warning to me not to speak out against him at this meeting."

Charlie watched the effect of this sweep across their faces. He saw Lynn, looking pinched and anxious, in the back. Ida Jacobs stood up to say, "But I've seen them together a lot. Robbie likes John."

Charlie held up his hand. "You haven't heard the worst. The man he shot was supposed to have been armed with a knife. A homemade knife, and very unusual. Three days before the shooting, I saw the same knife in Mack's desk. Now how do you explain that?"

There was a silence. Then Phil Julian asked, "Didn't you take this information to the police?"

"Yes, I did, and I learned that John Mack shot another man in very similar circumstances only four years ago. Two killings. Both shot in the heart. This man kills people. Do you see that?"

Fran Jeffries stood up and started for the door. Charlie said, "Fran, are you leaving?"

She stopped and turned toward him. Her eyes glittered with anger. "Yes, I am. That man's the best thing that ever happened to this building. I was ready to move out. I stayed because of him. And I resent the fact that he's not here to defend himself."

Charlie answered sharply, "That was his choice. I asked him to be here."

"Did you? Well, I doubt it was a very warm invitation. I'll just cast my vote now, and it's no, Charlie, no, I don't want John Mack fired. Now, good night."

She left, closing the door sharply. Charlie looked helplessly at Phil Julian. Julian responded by asking, "But are the police going to investigate this knife thing?"

"No, they're not. They say it could be coincidence. It's not important to them. It's open season on junkies . . . you just have to make sure your license is in order."

"Charlie, what are you talking about? I think you're worried about your kid." Dr. Julian stood up. "Why don't we wait until Robbie's back safe, and then we can take another look at this. You've given us a lot to consider, and I don't think we can just turn our back on your feelings, but, you know, most people are willing to go along with the police . . ."

Sue Kramer stood up behind Julian and cut through his hesitation. "I agree with Hyatt," she said. "I think he's dangerous." She went on to tell how Mack had muscled a key away from one of her boyfriends. Looking at the faces of the other tenants, Charlie could see they didn't care. He wished the Chamberses were here. Bob Chambers saw through Mack.

As soon as Sue was finished, Ida Jacobs was up. "But John told us not to pass keys out. He said that was the most important thing of all."

Sue was back on her feet. "But that's exactly the point, Mrs. Jacobs. How can we let this man come in here and tell us how to live?"

"I don't care," Ida Jacobs said passionately. "I feel safe with John around. I *know* he'll take care of things."

Charlie was dismayed to hear a murmur of agreement. He took the floor again. "Hasn't anyone been listening? This man is dangerous. I'm not a shrinker, but I can spot a nut, and John Mack's got something seriously wrong with his head. As long as you're passive with him, he's fine. Sure, he lets the maid in and out and he packs up the groceries, but if you buck him you quickly begin to see a very different man. You folks didn't see Rudy Simbro in the hospital. I did. His face looked like hamburger."

"Charlie," Phil Julian said, "isn't that beside the point? I think you have to give us a little time on this. We'll all keep our eyes open, and if there's another incident, we'll meet again."

"I want him out," Charlie said stubbornly.

Claire Julian rose to join her husband. "Charlie," she said gently. "We live here too, and it seems that most of us don't agree with you." Claire turned to look back at Lynn. "How do you feel about this?"

Lynn shook her head. "Leave me out of it."

Morrison took the floor. "I kind of agree with Hyatt that the bastard's got a strange smell. I soldiered myself, and I know the type. But you've got to admit he's efficient, and I was there the day he shot the prowler. I was right behind him, and he didn't have time to go down in the basement and get a knife out of his desk. So he would have had to be carrying it, right? Does that make sense? Why would he be carrying around a homemade knife?"

"I don't know," Charlie said uncertainly. "He's an odd man."

Morrison hadn't sat down. "The way I see it, he's doing the job, and if we fire him we're right back where we started. It wasn't one of us that got killed—"

"Jesus!" Charlie said passionately. "That's exactly what I'm talking about. Because he keeps us safe, are we going to look the other way when he kills someone?"

At this moment, there was the sound of the front door being opened, and Charlie automatically paused and looked around. Robbie came in. His eyes widened with surprise when he saw the meeting. Then he nodded at Charlie and started for his bedroom.

When Charlie looked back at the meeting, he saw clearly that he had lost them. Mr. and Mrs. Jacobs and the new people, the Andriolas, were getting up to leave. Phil Julian put his hand on Charlie's arm. "Look, we'll talk about this tomorrow night." Behind Julian, Charlie saw Lynn leaving the room, and he knew she was going back to see how Robbie was. The meeting was over, and nothing had been decided. Morrison stopped to talk to Charlie on the way out.

"Having that guy here," Morrison said, "is like having our own private police force. I mean, we know the cops take bribes, sell dope, and beat up suspects, but they don't do it to us." Morrison smiled as if that settled everything, and Charlie was suddenly too weary to try to argue. He saw everyone out and went down the hallway to Robbie's room.

Lynn had been talking to Robbie, and the boy

looked up with some anxiety when his father entered the room. Suddenly the frustrations of the meeting and the whole rotten, anxious day washed over Charlie, and he took two quick steps and slapped Robbie.

"Charlie!" Lynn said.

Robbie collapsed into tears. "He said it was all right, Dad . . ."

"Mack told him *you* said he could go," Lynn added.

"What are you talking about?"

"John told me you and he had talked out your differences, and that you said he could take me to see the Mets. That's all we did. We went to a ball game and then had dinner. That was all it was. He told me it was all right."

"Oh, Jesus, Robbie . . ." Charlie pulled his son into his arms. "I'm sorry."

He saw Lynn's face over Robbie's shoulder. She looked both relieved and troubled. "That motherfucker," he said to her. "He's some piece of work."

"Charlie," she said, "please let it go."

"Not a chance," he said. "Robbie, where did you leave Mack?"

Robbie drew back. His eyes were swollen with tears. "At the subway stop. He was going home."

CHAPTER SIXTEEN

Charlie tried several cabs before he found one that would take him to Queens. "As long as it's not Harlem," the driver said, with a tough grin. Charlie settled behind the plastic screen that was supposed to protect the driver from robbery. The plastic was stained and cracked and the slot for the money was broken out. They headed up 10th Avenue and across 125th Street. They took the Triboro bridge to the Grand Central Parkway, heading towards Astoria. At one point the driver asked, "You live out this way?"

Charlie was too angry to make talk. "No," he said shortly. The driver shrugged and turned on his radio.

Charlie stared out the window, watching the streets gradually deteriorate. Winter damage had not been patched, the cab bucked and wrenched over the pot-holes, and as they continued he saw more and more burnt out and abandoned buildings as if a battle had raged. Stripped and gutted car, wheelless hulks, slouched at the curbs and the street lights were blocks apart. The few walls that were illuminated showed an intricate and scribbled tangle of graffiti—names, boasts, obscenities—and high on the side of a brick warehouse someone had painted in large rude white letters: THE DEAD BOYS.

At several intersections he saw the nightlights of local juice bars and the crowds of young couples in the streets, dressed for disco, standing around their cars and motorcycles. He remembered it was Saturday night, the big night in the blue-collar world.

"How much farther?" he asked.

"At least ten minutes."

Charlie seldom thought about Queens. It was there, his friends knew it was there, but whoever came out here? It was much larger than he had imagined. The cab passed block after block after block of small box-shaped houses, seemingly identical in the poor light, all with storm doors and storm windows, each with its patch of lawn. When they finally stopped it was in front of one of these houses. A corner house, better cared for than most. A stain of yellow light illuminated the windows on the bottom floor. The meter stood at $18.75, and when Charlie had paid and tipped, he had less than $10.00 left in his pocket.

He hesitated and looked around. He saw no one on the street.

The cabbie asked, "You want me to wait?"

"No, I'm okay."

Charlie started up the walk as the cab rolled off. The long ride, the strange neighborhood, the quiet house in front of him, all drained some of the heat of his anger. He squared his shoulders and rang the bell. He heard it sounding inside, thin, tremulous. Immediately a dog began to bark. A big dog. Charlie heard its nails on the floor as it crossed the room inside to hurl itself against the door. Frantic to get at Charlie. It continued to bark and leap against the door for several minutes, and even after it stopped he could hear it inside still growling.

Obviously Mack wasn't home. Charlie stepped off the porch and walked into the shadows beside the house to peer into the window where the light was on. He saw dishes on the table where someone had eaten. A cardboard milk carton stood beside them. A television was drawn up where it could be seen from the table, but it was dark. On the other side of the room there was a workbench with tools racked above it. It took the dog only moments to catch on. It erupted into the kitchen, a big black-and-white longhair, and raced across the room to snap and bark at the window. Charlie stepped back.

"Hey, mister."

The voice came from the sidewalk behind him and Charlie turned around, feeling vaguely guilty, to find a small black boy, wearing one of those wool stocking caps that they were all affecting, and a jacket sizes too large. He looked about six except he had the expression of a bitter 15 year-old.

"Lock yourself out?"

"No," Charlie said and then went on to volunteer more than he intended. "I have to see the man who lives here, but he's not home." Charlie smiled as he asked, "Is there a pay phone around here?"

179

He walked across Mack's lawn as the boy told him, "At the shopping center."

"Where's that?"

The boy held his hand out in a universal gesture. The palm says fill me. This poor kid had been taught to sell courtesy. Well, why not, Charlie thought, as he found a quarter to hand to the boy. The boy barely glanced at the coin. His bitter expression deepened. He turned slowly and pointed across the street and up the block.

"Two blocks this way. You hang a right."

"Okay. Thanks."

Charlie started out, swinging his arms, trying to appear like a busy and cheerful man. The sharp sound of his heels on the pavement made him feel resolute. He walked along the row of unchanging houses, looking at the equally similar cars parked solid against the curb. A bumper strip caught his eye. It asked: *Where will YOU spend Eternity?* The YOU was in red caps and the center of the O was formed by a question mark. At the corner he passed a tiny grocery, locked up as tight as an armored car. In the next block, some instinct caused him to glance behind. The boy was 30 steps away.

"Are you following me?"

The boy frowned scornfully. "Nah, I live right over there."

Charlie found the shopping center closed, only a few cars still parked on the large lot. The whole area was lit with the harsh silver glow of large carbon arcs. It seemed strangely lifeless, and as he crossed the lot towards the phone booths on the far side, Charlie realized how much he had been hoping he'd find something open.

His mood darkened still further when he found the

phone booths both trashed. The receivers had been cut off, the coin boxes pryed out, and the phone books ripped up and scattered. He stared at the wanton and mindless damage as if it were personal. Like savages, he thought, and in that moment he knew he was going home. He could face Mack tomorrow. He thought of the subway, swaying as it raced under the river towards Manhattan.

But when he stepped out of the ruined phone booth, he found the black boy standing only ten feet away, looking up at him with the same bitter expression. "What do you want?" Charlie demanded angrily. "Another quarter?"

It was then he heard a murmur of laughter behind him and turned swiftly to find four more black kids spreading out around him. They had moved in silently in their sneakers. The oldest was no more than seventeen, and the youngest might have been thirteen. Still boys. And they were unarmed. They all wore army fatigue jackets, and the same wool stocking caps, pulled over their ears, except the leader who was already above 6 feet and slender as a bow; he was wearing a dark red beret.

"Say, man," the leader said in a soft exaggerated slur, "tha's right, you duke a quarter on that po liddle black boy." Several of the others smiled.

Charlie moved quickly, pushing the six-year-old to the side, as he began to run towards the street. He heard them behind him like a pack. He gained the sidewalk and headed towards the corner, hoping to find something open around the corner. He could already feel the effort of running and he was beginning to pant. Then two more boys, in the same fatigue jackets, stepped from behind a truck, just ahead. Charlie stopped, and turned around. The other boys came running up to ring him in. The leader was smiling.

"Now you still ain't give this po liddle black boy his quarter." He spoke in the same slurred parody of polite speech and Charlie could only spread his hands to ask what they wanted from him.

The leader went on, "Don't you know a quarter don't even buy a candy bar no more?"

"All right," Charlie said, trying to keep his own tone easy. "This is all I have." He took out his billfold and removed four Ones and a Five. He held them out, but the leader just stared at the money. "It's all I have. Really," Charlie said. "I have plastic, but you guys can't use plastic."

The leader nodded. "Oh, yes, we uses plastic. We don't never travel without it."

Charlie stripped his credit cards and added them to the money.

The leader adjusted his revolutionary beret, getting it at just the right angle over his eyes. "We tells time, too," he said.

As he removed his wrist watch, Charlie found himself wondering why this kid was out here playing street punk, when he was just the kind of smart and good looking young black the inner city people were looking for. Charlie added his watch to the pile and held it out.

Oddly, the leader took a half step back and folded his arms. "Now why don't you stick that loot up your pale gray ass?"

Charlie faltered and a spasm of fear took him. "I don't understand."

"TeeKay," the leader said, and the small black boy who had first followed Charlie stepped forward and unzipped his large jacket. He began to remove some

182

lengths of pipe from his belt and hand them around. They were old-fashioned metal pipes, handles had been formed by wrapping them with friction tape. Just like the handle of the shank. Charlie turned to look at the boys waiting behind him. One had a knife and the other held a length of chain.

Charlie turned back to see the leader coming towards him, slapping his pipe into the heel of his palm with a soft smacking sound. He stopped a yard from Charlie and leaned forward.

"Now you want to go home, don't you?"

Charlie understood this game was in earnest and he answered seriously, "Yes, I do."

"Yes, I know you do, and you don't live nowhere around here. We don't get your kind too often. Why, I bet you paid more for them shoes than my mama pays for a month's rent."

Charlie kept silent.

"Okay, you want to go, it's easy. You just get a bone on and you can go."

"I don't understand," Charlie said again. He heard the boys behind him laughing.

The leader continued with obvious relish. "Just get your johnson stiff. That's all."

The moment he comprehended, Charlie's scrotum shriveled. The weakness he felt was awful. "Oh, jesus," he said. "How do you think up shit like this?"

"Why, that's all we do. Haven't you heard? Now you get a bone on for me. I want to see that little white cock of yours just sticking up in those hundred dollar slacks."

It was the last thing Charlie could do. "I can't. You know I can't."

"No, I don't know that at all. You people are great fuckers. You fuck everyone. Just let your pants down

183

so we can all get a better look at that liddle thing when it comes up. You better do it."

Charlie couldn't. He put his hands to his belt, but he couldn't unbuckle.

The leader went on in the same soft tones. "Maybe we got to help you. You ever think how much your nuts are really more like grapes. Just a liddle soft pair of grapes." He slammed his pipe into his palm twice.

Abruptly, Charlie burst into tears. This was more than he could bear. "Please leave me alone," he said as he began to drop slowly to his knees. He knew that nothing he could say to this bitter boy would mean a thing. All he could do was plead. He lowered his head and continued to cry, kneeling there on the pavement. Then he heard a different voice.

"Mr. Hyatt?"

He raised his head. Standing out in the street, fifteen feet away from the ring of boys, was John Mack. He was wearing his same grey suit and his hat was pulled low over his eyes. He carried a paper bag full of groceries. Charlie's first feeling was a rush of gratitude. Then he realized he was kneeling in tears in front of a bunch of kids.

"You need some help, Mr. Hyatt?"

"Yes!"

John Mack put down his bag of groceries, and ran swiftly towards one of the cars parked at the curb. The boys shifted to watch him, but still guarded Charlie. Mack opened the driver's door, did something at the wheel, and the horn began to blare. Then he came around the car straight at the boys. The boys startled and began to back away. Mack put the nearest one down with a smart chop to the neck, and went straight for the leader. The leader tried to use his pipe, but Mack stepped around it, seized his arm, and came up behind him. The pipe fell to the sidewalk. Charlie saw the boy's mouth open in agony. Mack had him down with his arm driven up into the small of his back, and with his other hand Mack had scooped up the pipe. The horn continued to sound.

"You boys better get home," Mack said.

The boys looked at each other. Without their leader they were suddenly less certain. One of them made a feint at Mack, but he was careful not to get too close. Another kicked Charlie in the side. Charlie struggled to get to his feet. Up the street he saw a porchlight come on. The horn had pulled someone. The boys saw this.

"Better get moving," Mack said. "The crushers will be coming."

The boys began to back away. Suddenly they turned and ran. Charlie looked around. The only one left was the same little boy who had decoyed him in the first place. He gestured at the leader, still pinned by Mack, and said, "He's my brother."

Mack released the older boy, who sat up, rubbing his arm. He stared up at Mack, all the humor gone from his face. "I see you from time to time," he said.

"Make sure that's all you do," Mack said. "Now get out of here before I bust you up." He turned as if dismissing the two boys. "Are you okay, Mr. Hyatt?"

Charlie studied Mack's eyes and saw nothing but earnest concern. "I'm okay, I think."

The leader stood up, adjusting his beret. For the first time Charlie noticed the beginning of a mustache. "You're a lucky man," he said.

"Get out of here!" Mack snapped. "You kids are like vermin. Fucking lice. And keep out of my way." As the two boys walked off, it was the little one who stared back malevolently. Mack said to Charlie, "You have to be careful around here. Even the crushers are afraid of these kids. There's a dozen rat packs right in this neighborhood." Mack went out into the street to disengage the horn, and pick up his groceries. "You better come over to my place. I have to feed my dog. We can have a cup of coffee while I call you a cab."

"I don't have the fare," Charlie said.

"I'll loan you the money." Mack smiled as he went on. "I know you're good for it."

Charlie stiffened, but he couldn't imagine walking these streets looking for the subway. He started after John Mack, like a boy trailing his father.

CHAPTER

SEVENTEEN

The radio told Ida Jacobs it was going to be another hot, wet day, and she decided to go to the park even earlier than usual. She gathered the leftover bread, the heels and the crusts, and sacked it in a baggie, and then went into the bedroom to get the novel she was reading. She moved slowly, favoring her left leg. Down in the lobby she was pleased to find John Mack. He always looked nice in the morning when his shirt was still fresh and his jaw clean. He smiled as he greeted her.

"Good morning, Ida."

"Good morning, John. The radio says more heat, so I'm going early."

"That's a good idea. How's your leg?"

"A little better."

"Did you try those Epsom salts, like I told you?"

Ida hadn't. It was simpler to suffer with her leg than try to treat it. She looked vague, but brightened again when the front door opened and Mrs. Andriola came in with a bottle of soap powder. "Hi, John," Mrs. Andriola said.

Mack nodded, still smiling. "How's that faucet?"

"Just fine."

Mrs. Andriola started up the stairs, passing Charlie Hyatt, on his way down. Hyatt was dressed for work, suit and tie, and he was carrying his brief case. When he saw John Mack he stopped for a moment. Then came over. Ida watched him take a twenty dollar bill from his pocket and hand it to John. "I've been meaning to get this back to you."

John nodded, "That's okay, sir, I wasn't worried about it."

Ida looked from one man to the other and began to feel uncomfortable. She didn't like the way they were looking at each other.

Mack spoke again. "Is everything okay?"

"Yes," Charlie Hyatt said. Then he smiled tightly and added. "Well, I'm running late."

Ida watched the door close behind Mr. Hyatt, and she couldn't shake her sense of trouble. "John," she said thoughtfully, "do you suppose Mr. Hyatt's not well? He used to seem so cheerful all the time, but here lately—" She paused, uncertain what it was she sensed.

John Mack said, "I believe he's got family troubles."

"Oh," Ida said. "Is it his—"

John Mack laughed and patted her on the arm. "Ida, I can't gossip about the tenants. Come on, now, I'll walk you over to the park. Maybe if we're lucky we'll see a few cardinals."

THE WHIPPING BOY

a novel by
Beth Holmes

THE WHIPPING BOY is a brilliant and often terrifying portrait of 12-year-old Timmy Lowell and his parents, Evie and Dan. They were a "model" middle class family—until they realized that Timmy, their first-born, was slowly turning into a psychotic killer. His father, locked into his own terrifying world, cannot help him; can't see the evil seed growing. Only Timmy's mother, Evie, can save him...or become his next victim.

jove

$2.50   K12046983
Available wherever paperbacks are sold.

NT-37